IVAN

House of Frazier Book 5

KATHI S. BARTON

This is a work of fiction. Names, characters, places, and incidents are products of the author's imagination or are used fictitiously and are not to be construed as real. Any resemblance to actual events, locations, organizations, or persons, living or dead, is entirely coincidental.

World Castle Publishing, LLC
Pensacola, Florida

Copyright © 2026 Kathi S. Barton
Hardback ISBN: 9798242346512
Paperback ISBN: 9798891265042
eBook ISBN: 9798891265059
First Edition World Castle Publishing, LLC, January 19, 2026
http://www.worldcastlepublishing.com

Licensing Notes

Cover: Cover Designs by Karen
Editor: Karen Fuller

Chapter 1

Devlin kept an eye on his client. Serenity Rangers was so calm, but he had a feeling that on the inside, she was raging hot. Her mother. If you knew the two of them, you'd understand that statement right away, he thought. But her mother was a narcissistic bitch who needed someone to take her to task in a big sort of way. Not only that, but it wouldn't hurt the older woman to be put away someplace that she couldn't bother others. She was royally pissing off her daughter. And he understood now why Sen was asked to bring an attorney with her when she came to the reading of the will.

"I was his sister. Why didn't he leave me more than just a little bit of money?" The attorney for the firm that was reading the will pointed out that she was left with ten thousand dollars. Not a paltry sum by any means. "But he left her all the rest of the money. How is that fair when I was his sister?"

He was reasonably sure that the furniture in the large conference room understood that she was his sister; she'd said it so many times now. Devlin's head was killing him, and he'd only been sitting here for the last hour and a half. He couldn't understand how someone could live with her and not have all sorts of ailments.

"Ms. Debra Ranger, that's the extent of the will reading for you. You may wait in the lobby or go home. There is no more reason for you to wait around for the rest." Debra asked if there was more money going to her daughter. "There is no reason for you to know what else is in the will unless Ms. Serenity wants you to know."

"Mother, just go. If there is anything else, I'll let you know. We just have to clear away the house in my name and the money that he left me." She said she should have gotten the house. "Well, I guess he figured that you had one and didn't need anything else. Just go, please, before I have a migraine again and have to go to the doctors. That will delay me getting to talk to you, too."

"All right, but you take notes on what you get. That way, I can sue you for it later. There is no point in you getting more than I did because he was—"

"Yes, mother, he was your brother. And since everyone knows that now, you don't have to keep repeating it. Just go home, and I'll call you later. If I'm not sick. You know how I get when I have a migraine." She said she didn't want to be around her when she was throwing up again. "Like you ever hung around when I was sick anytime in my life. Just go, please."

After Debra left, huffing and puffing about wills and money the entire time, Sen asked for ten minutes so that she could go to the bathroom and stave off her headache. Devlin felt sorry for the young woman and wanted to help her, so he was going to do his best to make sure that things were settled for her before he left her. Things would just need to be filed, and he might even do that for her; he felt that badly for her. When she came back, she looked as if she'd been crying, and he wanted to protect her from her mother. The woman was a terrible person to be around.

"I'm all right now. You said that he left me their home. I'm most excited about that." The attorney for the firm he was there with said that now that her mother was gone, he could talk business with her. "You mean I don't get the house? I'm sorry. I've been under a little bit of stress." That was an understatement if he'd ever heard one.

"Your uncle knew that your mother would be... let's just say he knew your mother well and wanted to have her out of the room when the rest of the will was read. There's quite a bit more to it than the small house they lived in. They both did very well for themselves, and in turn, you as well. The two of them left you a vast estate. And it all goes to you." Sen said she didn't understand. "They had houses all over the country and the world. There is money enough for you to enjoy a very happy life without ever having to work again. In addition to the house they lived in, there is jewelry, land, and money totaling up to be in the billions. They invested well and were lucky in the stock market, too."

"I'm sorry. Did you say they left me millions of dollars?" The man shook his head and said he'd said billions. "Billions with a b? My uncle and aunt left me billions of dollars when they died, and I'm somehow supposed to keep this from my mother? I think I'd have better luck cutting my arm off and her not noticing it. She's dense but not stupid."

"He didn't want you to keep it from her. He just wanted you to know what you were to get when you were alone with an attorney. As I said, he knew how your mother would be and that would have been difficult for you to have been able to understand what the will entails with her around. I'm sorry, but I do believe he had the right of it." Sen nodded and said he was right. "You may tell her or not. She already knows you got the house and the rest of the estate. Your mother just has no idea how large the estate is until you wish to tell her. If you do at all."

"She'll sue me for it, too." Devlin told her that he'd make sure that things went her way if it came to that. "I know that, and you know that, but it won't stop her from suing me. And she'll expect to be able to visit all the homes, too. Billions of dollars, you said?"

"Yes, my dear. There are billions of dollars when everything is totaled up." She didn't seem to be upset about the money so much as she was about her mother finding out. Not that he blamed her. The woman was going to cause all kinds of trouble when she did, too. He had a feeling that suing her daughter would be the least of Sen's problems with her mother. "If you're ready, we can begin to read the rest of the will so that you can have a better grip on what was left to you and the terms of the agreement."

"So there's a catch." He said only in that she had charities that needed to be taken care of as well. "So that money I have goes to them."

"How about we just let him read the will, and we'll go from there. It might be that he has other money that goes to the charities that isn't a part of your estate." The attorney said that was true. "See. Let's just get through this, and you'll have a better understanding of what he wants you to do with some of the money that he's left behind for you to take care of."

By lunch time, the will had been gone over, and while he'd been taking notes, he noticed too that Sen did as well. She would also write down questions that she had as they went over the will, and he was quite proud of her. Being dropped into a situation like she had been, she was doing very well. The firm provided lunch to the three of them. It was just the break that Sen needed to get her shit together, as his big brother was forever saying about people.

"There is a lot to do when you suddenly have money, isn't there?" He said that he thought people with money who knew how to keep it had a lot to do. "I want to keep it all, but I know I'm going to have difficulties doing that. I don't know the first thing about investments."

"There is a firm here at the office that does that for you. He did it for your aunt and uncle and was said to be able to do that for you as well." She said she'd forgotten about that. "That's fine. You're doing very well. I had no idea there was so much to the estate, or I might have brought more paper with me to take notes. I'm glad to see that you are as well."

"I don't know how to do anything without taking notes. It's what makes me a good clerk for Judge Rainer. I wonder if he knew." He said that he would imagine that he did know. "I guess. He was really good about not giving me a heads-up. My mother would have found out. I have a feeling that my family wouldn't have wanted Mom to know. I can understand that, too. She would have drained them dry before the ink was dry on the paperwork. I'm going to do the same thing, I think."

"Good for you. If I can help you in any way

after this, you need only to call me. Or if you have any questions about what you've been told. I would love to be there for you." He had a feeling that she'd call too. Not that she was stupid or anything like that, but because she'd get home and think about things and have questions for him. Devlin found he didn't mind at all. "Now he'll go over the estate part, where you'll have to keep up with his charities. There aren't that many, but they'll need to be kept on top of. That shouldn't be hard to do with the same firm for your investments. I'd get with them and see if you can learn what they're doing so that you can make sound judgments when it's time for you to decide on things."

"I will. That's a good idea." When she finished eating, he noticed that she neatly put her plate back on the stack of dirty ones. She was neat about everything that she did, he noticed, even taking her notes. "I'm a little overwhelmed right now. I know it'll get better down the road, but right now all I can think of is how much there is to everything. My mother would have a fit if she were to find out about how vast this estate is. Then she'd want to spend it."

"I did notice that about her. Does she work?" She said she's been retired from life for a while now. "I'm not sure I know what that means."

"Sometimes I don't either. She never worked, as far as I know, but she seems to have money when she wants something. Or she tries to take mine. I live all right, but when she comes around and wants me to treat her to a day of things, I run a little short. I guess I don't have to worry about that anymore. I have become really good at telling her no." He nodded as if he understood. And he did to a point. The more time he spent with Debra, the more he thought she was like his own mother. He wondered if she'd ever hit on Sen. He wouldn't put it past her. Not like his mother beat them, but just hit her around enough to keep her in line with the way she was thinking. "I guess we're ready to start again. I'm actually having fun here today. It's something I've never done before, and I'm having a blast."

"I'm glad you are. It's good to see you smiling." He thought of how he wanted to protect her from people like her mom and thought that was silly of himself. He'd protect her from people like her mom without any trouble, he supposed, but it still bothered him that she had that effect on him. Not bothered, but it was weird that he did. "I have this brother that you should meet. He's a vet. I think that the two of you would hit it off great. He's neat as a pin, like you are."

"I don't get out much. I don't remember the last time I had a date. I'm forever working, and I love my job. Judge Rainer takes really good care of his staff." He said that he knew him from college. "Yes, he teaches there a few days a week. I help him with that as well sometimes when he needs it."

"Have you thought of being an attorney? With the knowledge that you have, I'd bet you'd be a shoo-in." She said she could certainly afford to become one now. "That you can." They both laughed, and he sat down where he'd been sitting before the break.

"No, as for being an attorney, I don't think I'd like that. I'm not lazy or anything, but it seems like a lot of work to put into it for something that I don't think I'll like. I enjoy clerking for the judge, but that's about the extent of my law classes I want to take. You'd have to be dedicated all the time, and I want to do things when I'm off work. Don't you ever just want to be free of your tie and job?"

"Some days more than others. Not today. It's nice having someone who isn't guilty of something trying to get off." They both thought that was funny and were still laughing when David, he finally remembered his name, came back in the room with them. They still had a lot to go over, it seemed.

By the time they were finished, it was coming up on four o'clock. His mind was full, and he was sure that Sen was still as overwhelmed as she had been. But she was polite in thanking him for his help. The next thing he talked to her about was filing her name on everything that she had. He said he could do that for her as soon as next week. She was fine with that.

"The next thing you should do is fill out a will. You have a lot of things that need to be done with your newfound wealth, and you don't want to leave it to just anyone. I'd get on that soon so that it's taken care of." She asked him if she had to leave it all to her mother. "No. There is nothing that says you have to leave it to a relative at all. You can leave your money to whomever you wish. Is there something to do with your mother that you don't want to include her in your will? Something that I should be looking out for?"

"I don't know why that popped into my head like it did. It was as if you said that I needed a will, and I thought of her knocking me off for my money." She shook her head. "I'm sorry. She's never beaten me before, but that's a great deal of money that wasn't left to her. And I'm going to not tell her either. But if she were to find out…"

"You just have to be careful." She nodded, and he was more worried for her than he was before. "I'd not tell her if I were you. You don't have to tell her anything other than you were left the house and some money to make sure that it's kept up with. If she finds out, then deal with that when it happens."

"I will and thank you again for your help today. I might still have questions, but for now, I think I got it. I'll just have to take it one day at a time." She smiled at him, and he felt that overwhelming need to protect her again. "I'll call you if I have any questions for sure. Thanks again."

As he made his way home, he wanted to go by Ivan's house and see if he smelled funny to him again. The last time he'd been around her, Ivan said he smelled of sunshine or something along those lines. It was weird how he wanted this woman in his life but knew that she wasn't his mate. Time would tell, he supposed. But he was going to get the two of them together.

~*~

"I think you should allow me to live in the house with you. That way, I can keep track of you." Her mom had been hounding her all evening about the house and money she told her that she got. "I'm going to put the money on my house so that I can borrow against it to buy me something bigger. I've always wanted a bigger house than your uncle and his wife."

"His name is Robert, and her name is Cindy. Please get it right." Her head was beginning to hurt worse, and it had all to do with her mother. "I told you everything that I know. And no, you're not living with me in the house. You have one, stay there. I want to live in the house alone and enjoy my solitude."

"Why are you so selfish all the time? It's just a little house, and you should want to take care of me. I took care of you when you were little." She explained to her for the fifth time that she'd been taken care of by nannies and had been in boarding school when it was time for her to go to school. "Well, I had to be there when you got home, didn't I? It wasn't always nannies and fun times for me, you know."

"No, you got to claim a daughter that you had nothing to do with until I was older." Her mother didn't like that, and she found that she didn't care. "I'm going to be moving into the house over the next couple of weeks. After that, I'm going to make sure that I live alone for the rest of my life and work to make that happen. I don't want you as a roommate. I have enough going on without you right up in my face all the time."

"Well, aren't you a selfish bitch. I see how you are. You get yourself some money and a house, and you're suddenly too good to hang out with your own mother. I'm guessing that Robert left you secure in the house, too, didn't he? Did he tell you to change the locks on the house? I have a key, you know. I got it once when he wasn't aware. Fat lot of good it did me. They were forever home and never went anywhere, so I could get in. That's just selfish of them, too. They had that nice place and wouldn't allow me to live there with them either."

"You hated Aunt Cindy. Why on earth would

you want to live there with them?" She said she got bored living alone. "Well, you're going to have to get used to it because you're not living with me. And I've already had the locks changed before I left the attorney's office. He suggested it because I didn't know who had keys."

"Selfish is all you've ever been, all your life. I don't even know why I bother with you anymore. You never want to take me out." She pointed out that she had money now to burn. "But you should be treating me to those things. I'm your mother, aren't I?"

"Yes, you are. But I'm an adult now and need my own privacy. I like my own company too. So live in your house, and I'll live in mine. It's the way it should be." Mother huffed and stomped her foot. "That won't do you a bit of good. I've made up my mind, and I'm going to stick to it. You have your own money from the estate. Enjoy it while it lasts."

"Then you'll allow me to live with you." She said that she was never living with her. "Why not? Damn it, Sen, you never were a good daughter to me. I just want you to allow me to live with you so that we can have fun together."

"You want me to spend my money on you, and I have to keep it for taxes and such in owning a new to me home." She told her that she'd never paid taxes. "Then how are you living in that house without getting into trouble?"

"I don't know, and I don't care so long as I can do it. You should find yourself a nice, rich husband and have him take care of the taxes so that you and I can have mother-daughter dates. That would be fun, wouldn't it?" She said that she didn't want to find a rich husband. "With your all right looks, it shouldn't take much to find yourself one."

"It's time for you to leave now." Her mother said she'd only just gotten there. "You've been here too long. I've had enough of you picking at me, and it's time you left. I have to go to work tomorrow, so I don't want to see you for the rest of the week. Go do whatever you want with your money and leave me alone."

"Well, I never." She could feel a headache coming on and didn't want to deal with it with her mother. "You might call me up one of these days, and I won't want to have anything to do with you. See how that will make you feel."

"I'll take my chances." As soon as her mother left, she put the chain on the door. If she convinced the landlord that she was able to get in again, she wanted something to slow her down. To think that she'd been feeling bad because her mother had been left out of the will, but for the ten grand that she'd gotten from the estate. "She's the one who his selfish. I've never been around anyone like her in my life. I hope she doesn't want to have fun with me again."

Her uncle and aunt had died just a little over a month ago. Her uncle had had a massive heart attack and died when he plowed into the back of a bunch of cars while driving, and that had killed her aunt by nearly decapitating her in the process. Since they were organ donors, they had come to the hospital with life support on them so that they could donate their organs and eyes. They had saved six people with that, and three people were now able to see because of the donation.

Her mother had known for two weeks that they'd been in the accident and hadn't told her. She acted like it was no big deal for her to have had to pull the plug, her words, not Sen's, because she was tired of waiting on him to die. If that didn't make her mother selfish, she didn't know what did. There were days when she wished she were Uncle Roberts and Aunt Cindy's daughter rather than her mother's.

Going to lie down on her bed, she thought of moving. She could well afford to leave everything behind when she moved into the bigger house, but she had a few things that she wanted to keep. Not much. More than likely stuff that would fit in her car to take over. Since the other house was furnished, all she had to do was figure out what she wanted to keep and get rid of. She didn't think that there would be all that much that she didn't want, as they had very nice tastes in what they had around the house.

After taking a nap, she did feel better. Tomorrow, she was going to finish packing up her things to go to the other house and donate the rest of her things here. She could have gone right to the house to stay, but she wanted to make sure that the paperwork had been filed so that it was all hers. Devlin said he'd call her when it was filed away so that she'd not have to worry about it. The deeds to the rest of the property were going to be filed as well.

As if he knew she was thinking about talking to him, her cell phone rang, and it was him. He told her that not only had things been filed for her, but her bank account had been set up in her name. He also made sure that the insurance policies that were in her name were ready to be cashed out as well.

"I've made it so that the bank is aware that you don't want your mother to be able to get into your accounts. She's not even to know that you have an account at the same bank that your aunt and uncle had one." She told him that it was a brilliant idea. "I take it she's tried that with your accounts before."

"My uncle's too. He told her that he was going to have her arrested if she tried that again. I don't know whether he ever called the police on her or not, but he seemed really pissed off at the time. Even though she had no right to be upset, she didn't speak to him for months afterwards. She doesn't understand boundaries. She either doesn't understand or doesn't care. I've never figured that out yet." He asked her if she had any questions. "I believe you answered them all for today. I'm going to go to the new house in the morning. I've decided that I can afford to donate all the things that I don't want here."

"We have a charity that we buy up old and used furniture to have around for when people have a house fire or something along those lines. If you're going to donate it anyway, why not donate it to that?" She told him he could have everything, as the house she was getting was furnished. "Yes, it is. And while I haven't seen the house, I'm betting that it's in good shape for you to live in right away."

"That's what I'm thinking as well. That it'll be just the way they left it." She had a terrible thought of them dying and just realizing that they'd not be back anymore. "They were the greatest family I've ever had. I'm going to miss them so much. I wish I could have seen them one more time. Just so that I could tell them that I loved them once more."

"I'm so sorry for your loss, Sen. It must have been hard on you without your mother telling you that they'd been in an accident." She said that she'd known about it for two weeks and hadn't said a word. "I'm sorry. I wish I had known. I would have certainly said something to you about it."

"How could you have known. Only she knew, and she was a selfish person for not telling me." She asked him to forgive her for crying. "She gets me so upset. Did I tell you that she is mad at me because I won't allow her to live with me? Why, when she has her own house, would living with me be all right?"

"I don't know, honey." He told her how sorry he was again, then told her she was doing the right thing in having her mother not be able to get into her home. "That way, you can have peace and quiet around your home without worrying about her getting in when you don't expect her to be there."

"She'll figure out something, I've no doubt." When she looked up at the clock, she couldn't believe how long she'd kept him on the phone. "I should let you go. I know that I'm not your only client. Thank you for calling me, and I'm sorry that I cried on your shoulder. I'll do better the next time we talk." He told her not to worry about it. "I do. I don't want you to think that I'm someone who cries all the time. It's been a rough couple of weeks for me. A rough month."

"I understand. I really do. How about we go and get some dinner tonight? I would love to take you out for something special since you got your house in order again." She said she'd love that, but he didn't have to do that. "It'll be my pleasure. My brothers usually met up on Thursday night, but since the weather had two of them snowed in in another state, we put it off until next week again. How about a nice steak dinner? Maybe my brother Ivan will join us. He's been alone since the other two are gone."

"I'd love that if you're sure that I'm not intruding." He said he'd pick her up at five-thirty. "Great, I'll be ready then. Thank you for this. I need someone to take me out of my head for a couple of hours. You'll be perfect because I can ask you questions as I think of them."

"Great. Ivan will be in a good mood because he delivered ten puppies today while the dog was in for a checkup. He's a vet." She said she might want a puppy someday. "Good. He knows the best ones to get. You should get with him so that he can help you out."

After getting off the phone with him, she couldn't believe how good she felt. So much better than dealing with her mother. As she decided to get dressed up, she needed to get a shower. After that, she pulled out one of her few dresses and got ready. It was going to be nice being escorted to a restaurant by two gentlemen. She was really looking forward to getting out and doing something she wanted to do.

Chapter 2

Ivan didn't really want to go out with his brother and friend. He had shit to do at home that needed his attention, and going out to be a third wheel didn't sound like fun. He knew that he could pick her out of a lineup by her personality because Devlin had talked about her so much, but he just wanted to stay home. But he'd go because his brother didn't want his friend to think it was a date. He didn't know why he'd been thinking that, but this was Devlin, and who knew how his mind worked sometimes.

Since he'd told the woman that they'd be having steaks, he decided to wear a suit. He didn't get to wear one much, being the county vet, but he did like to dress up on occasion just to be dressed up. Tonight he was going to have a nice dinner with his brother, and if the girl didn't cause too much trouble, he'd be all right with her, too. Ivan really did have a lot to get done in his house.

He'd got two bedroom sets at the last auction, and he'd yet to get them put together. There were dressers that went with them that he had to clean up and polish nicely. They were lucky for him to be in the bedrooms that he wanted them in, but not even close to being ready to put together. They were dusty and needed to be polished up as well. Once he got them put together, the rooms would be ready, with the exception of a mattress set. He'd have to order them tomorrow once the beds were put together.

When Devlin picked him up, he noticed that he was dressed the same way he was in a nice suit that looked good on him. Ivan didn't have much use for a suit, but when Brandy, Lica's mate, came to the family, she made sure that all of them had a nice suit or two so that if needed, they'd have one. He used his for meetings and going to funerals. And that's all. He was sure that Devlin used his every day as he was the family attorney. He'd never seen Lica in one, so he had no idea if he wore them all that much. He probably did because Brandy was into a lot of things. Once his brother picked him up, he was feeling better about this non-date.

"She's a nice lady, just been dealt a shitting hand in her mother. She reminds me of our mother in that it all has to be about her. I don't think she's ever hurt her physically, but she does treat her badly when it comes to being mentally abused." Ivan asked what they were going to be going out a lot. "No. I'm hoping she's your mate."

"This is a setup? Take me home right now.

Damn it, Devlin. I don't want to be set up." He pointed out the other day how he'd been smelling flowers. "You must be wearing something flora. I smell it on you today, too. So what is it that you're wearing?"

"She hugged me. That's all, she just hugged me a couple of times, and that's why I smell like her." He said that might not be it. "Well, you won't know until you meet her. And the thing is, you and I will be the only ones who know. You have until the others get back to see if she's your mate or not. That should be enough time to convince her that you're a good guy and have no designs on her money. She's wealthy, too. Did I tell you that?"

"Should you tell me that?" He said probably not. "Sheesh, Devlin talk about breach of promise or whatever it's called."

"I shouldn't have told you, but I didn't want you thinking that she's after yours. I honestly don't know why I told you. I just feel really protective of this girl, and I'm hoping that she's your mate. She's not mine. Her mom is going to be trouble, so it would make me feel better to know that she has someone from the family in her corner." He pulled up in front of her apartment; he got out of the car to help her across the snowy steps. As soon as he was near the beautiful woman, he knew without a doubt that she was his other half. Looking at his brother when he got out of the car, too, Devlin backed off when he growled low in his throat. He might have only been helping, but she was his, and he wanted him not to touch her.

Dinner was a little tense at first. He didn't know what to do with this newfound information, and Devlin didn't seem to know what to do about her hugging him. After a few minutes, he settled down and no longer cared if his brother hugged her or not. He was just feeling good that she had found him.

After they ordered, he wanted to talk to her about her life with him from now on. He didn't mean that he was going to make her do things that she didn't want to, but he would make sure that her mother wasn't going to be bullying her again. He'd also make sure that no one hurt her ever again. He had a feeling from listening to Devlin that her mother hurt her heart all the time when she was around. He wanted to put a stop to that as well. If she would allow it.

When their plates were taken away, he was really enjoying himself. They'd talked about everything and anything while they ate, and he had learned through Sen that she was sitting on a billion dollars that she'd just inherited from her uncle and aunt.

"They were killed recently, and your brother has been helping me get things squared away. Mostly it's with the houses that they left me, but money too. I'm going to be moving into my new home as soon as tomorrow. All the locks have been changed, and I'm ready to start my new life without my mother around." He asked if she was that bad. "She will be if she finds out what I really got from my aunt and uncle."

"Are you planning on telling her?" She said it would be her luck that her mother would find out and try to take it all from her. "But she doesn't know now, correct?"

"No, I don't plan on telling her anything. But she'll figure it out is what has me so afraid. I don't know what she'll do; she already said that she was going to sue me if I did her wrong. I honestly don't know what she'll do for billions of dollars. Hurt me for sure to get it back from me." She looked around the restaurant, and he'd bet she wasn't seeing anything but whatever was going on in her mind. "She will hurt me. Will she kill me? I don't know. I really don't know that she wouldn't stoop that far to get the money that was given to me."

"She sounds dangerous." Sen turned and looked at him, and he could see the tears as they fell down her cheeks. "Oh, love, don't cry. I'll make sure that she doesn't hurt you. I'll protect you with my life, as will my family."

"I have no one to protect me. And I know you're just saying that, that you'll protect me. You don't know me. I'm just a stranger that you agreed to have dinner with because your brother bullied you into it. You're sweet. Handsome even, but we both know that if it came right down to it, you'd want to save your ass over my own." He told her that he'd die for her. "Die for me? You don't even know me."

"I know that you're afraid of your mother, and that hurts me too. I know…I know that you're my mate and that everything about you makes me want to be there for you. You're funny and articulate. You have a good sense of humor when it comes to having fun. You're wealthy beyond what I have, but I think we can still get along." He grinned. "I think you're the most beautiful creature that I've ever laid eyes on since I've been born."

"Mate?" He nodded. "I know what that means, but not in the context of you and me. You must be a shifter of some kind."

"Wolf. My brother Lica, the oldest of us, is the Alpha of our pack. And he's well respected, too. He and his mate run the pack very nicely since we've been getting help from some of the outside help." She asked him what sort of outside help, and he wished he hadn't said anything. "My brother Ayden got hit in the head by a baseball bat. Once that was done to him, he could see ghosts. I know that it's hard to believe, but it's the truth. Something else you should know is that I can never lie to you. Not that I would, but I can't."

"You can't ever lie to me?" She looked at Devlin, and he was nodding. "I've never known anyone who couldn't lie to me before. That would be kind of strange."

"What do you think about you being my mate for all time?" She told him that she had to think about that. It seemed like a big deal. "It is for us both. You'll get some magic too. I don't know what kind. You should be able to dress yourself with just a thought. I can do that now as well."

"When you shift, are you naked?" He said that he used to be before she came along. "Well, good for you. And me. I'm not ready to see you naked just yet. Where do you live?"

"I have a condo that's not far from here. I used to live in the same complex as Ayden did. They've all found themselves houses now and have left me there. The only one left is Devlin. But we don't live on the same end as each other." She said that he knew where she lived, and it was just temporary. "Yes, you live in your new home starting tomorrow. Have you been in it since they passed away?"

"I've not been in it since Christmas, when we were all there for the holiday. Well me and some of their friends. My mother decided that she had better things to do than to hang out with her brother and his wife. They never got along all that well. I'm sure nothing much has changed with it in the last couple of months. I have to clean it up, I suppose, but that'll be easy. I think they had someone come in and clean for them once or twice a week when they were still alive." He asked her if she was going to keep the staff. "I've not decided. I've only ever been in the living room and kitchen of the place, but I don't think it's all that big. I know that it had two bedrooms in it at the time when I was a child. But as they were always having it tinkered with, I have no idea what I'm getting from them. I know that I'll appreciate it for all time. I miss them."

"I bet you do." They talked about her aunt and uncle while Devlin took a phone call. As he walked away, the two of them seemed to be getting along nicely, and he wanted his brother to go away. He'd not tell him that; he didn't want to hurt his feelings, but he wanted to get to know his new mate. "How about your mother? I'm to understand that you're expecting trouble from her. Is that right?"

"Yes. I don't know what sort of trouble, but I know that if she finds out about how much money I got from the estate, she'll hurt me. She might try something more with me, but I just don't know." He asked if she'd been violent before. "Not physically, not since I left home the first time."

"So she'd hit you before. That's not good. I mean, as the years have gone by, has she threatened you in any way that you should take her seriously about?" She said she just didn't know; there had never been this money between them before. "And you're sure she's going to find out about it. Even though you won't tell her."

"Yes, simply because I don't want her to know. And she'll make a big deal about it and be pissed off with me. I've never been afraid of her before, but now all I can think about is what lengths she'll go to in order to harm me. And she will too when she finds out." He said that he'd keep her safe. "You can't be around me all the time, Ivan. You have a business to run, just as I do with my job. I can't allow you to be hurt because of her."

"I promise you I'll be there when you need me." She told him that was a big promise. "It is, and one that I plan on keeping too."

Devlin came back and said that he had an emergency to attend to. When he left them there, he realized that he didn't have a ride back home. Shaking his head at his brother, he told Sen that he'd figure something out for them, but they could start walking.

"It's not all that far, and we can talk while we walk. It's supposed to be in the upper seventies tomorrow, so it might be warm enough for us tonight." As soon as they left the restaurant, they realized two things. It was too cold to walk home, and her place was a lot closer than his was. "We can walk to your place, and I can call someone to come and get me. If that's all right with you."

"That's fine. I have a car. I can take you home. It won't be any trouble at all." She bundled up tighter and laughed. "I thought that we'd be having warmer nights by now. I never dreamed it would be this cold when we left my apartment."

"I should have driven myself." His brother reached out to him just as he was putting his gloves on. *"You left us stranded, dumbass."* They both laughed, and he said he was coming back to get them now. *"Don't do that. I'm headed to her place now, and she's going to take me home. It's cold, but we should be all right."*

"I'm so sorry. As soon as I got the call, I should have thought about how I'd driven. I don't know where my head was." He said that he was a good attorney and that's all he had thought of. *"I guess so. If you promise you'll both be all right, I'm going to head to Lica's place. They have a meeting in the morning about some guy who wants to merge his business with one of Brandy's. I don't think they're going to go for it, but I don't know."*

"We'll be fine. Also, I wanted to tell you thanks for setting me up. I couldn't be happier." His brother said he was glad that he really liked Sen. *"She's something else, but I think she's more worried about her mom than she wants to let on. I'll talk to you tomorrow when I get back home and warm up."*

After closing the connection, he told Sen what his brother had said. He left out the part of her being afraid of her mother, but he did want to know what could be done about her. They talked all the way to her apartment, and he was glad that she invited him in. He was a frozen wolf popsicle.

~*~

Debra didn't like that her daughter was keeping secrets from her, like the will-reading thing. She knew there had to be more to it than going over some paperwork. The house alone was worth more than she'd gotten in cash. She wanted her fair share, and Sen was going to be forking it over to her or she'd have to get even with her.

The house that she was living in had been a settlement between her and Sen's father. He said he'd keep her in a house so long as she lived for her not telling his wife that he'd had a one-night stand with her. It was working out well for her, but she wanted something more. It had been twenty-five years since Sen had been born, and it was about time that they talked again. She didn't think that he was smart enough to go against her, and while the house was nice and she didn't have to mess with things like paying taxes, she wanted something new. Something bigger than her daughter had. It was only fair.

She was sick of reminding people that he was her brother. By now, they should have understood that she should be the one who inherited everything and not her dumbass daughter. Sen wasn't smart enough to do anything right, and she'd always known that. She wanted what was rightfully hers, and that should have been everything.

Going to the bank, she decided that Sen would have been opening an account with whatever she got that she'd not. Standing in line wasn't something that she enjoyed and no matter how much she said loud enough for the person in front of her to hear, they wouldn't switch places with her. It was just a fucking question she had, and they were making it so that she didn't get the answers that she needed.

When she finally got up to the counter, the woman smiled at her. Trying her best not to be in a bad mood, she smiled back. After telling her that she wanted to get into her account, the woman seemed willing to help. Then she asked for identification.

"Well, it's my daughter's account. She lets me borrow from it on occasion. Just tell me how much is in the account, and I'll let you know how much I want to take out. Daughters are so nice to have around, aren't they?" The woman clicked on the keyboard and then looked at her. "Can't you find it? She had an account in here before. I just assumed that she'd put her money back in this bank. You see, my brother died, and I was to get the money, but she put it in her account. I just want what is coming to me."

"You want to borrow from it, or you want to take from it. That's a big difference. But it doesn't matter really. Without proper identification, I can't let you into her account." She explained that she was her mother. "And I understand that. You told me, but you're not on the account, so I can't allow you to take anything from the account."

"Well, the least you can do is tell me how much is in the account. You made me wait in line all this time. I tell you that Sen is going to be upset because I couldn't get into her banking account." She said that without proper identification, she wasn't getting any information. "Let me speak to your boss. I know that you have rules, but if I can speak to him, he'll let me into the account. I've gotten into her accounts before, and nobody put up a fuss about it. Just tell me the amount in it, and I'll be able to tell if she got money from my own brother's estate or not."

"I can't do that. The bank manager isn't going to allow you into her account either. There are notes on the account that tells that if anyone allows you into her account, even to know the amount, they will be sued. I don't need that kind of trouble going on with my life right now." She said that it would be just between the two of them. "I don't think so. I'm not even going to tell you that she has any accounts here."

"You already did that. What's one more bit of information? Come on. Just between us." The girl was signaling to have someone come to the window, and she turned to see that the security guard was coming toward them with his hand on his gun. "Are you kidding me right now? I just want the amount of the account. I don't know why you're calling the security cop over right now."

"Ma'am, is there a problem?" After explaining to the cop what she wouldn't do for her, Debra was asked to leave. "You're causing trouble in the bank, and that's never good. You should see your way out before I have to call in backup. We don't want any trouble around here."

"It's my brother's estate. I just know she's gotten more money than I did. She already got his house and all the crap he had in it. Cindy never did have a lick of decorating sense, and it shows throughout the house. Damn it, just tell me how much money she has in her account. That's all I wanted." She was being stared at, and she hated that. It wouldn't have been so bad if it were just a couple, but the entire bank was filled with people, some of them even had their phones out recording her. "Damn it, stop recording me. I demand that you stop that right now. It's my brother's estate, and I deserve it more than my stupid daughter does."

Debra found herself outside on the sidewalk after being dragged out of the building. She had lost her shoe. So when it was tossed out at her, she picked it up and was ready to throw it back at the man when she realized that people had come outside and were filming her still.

"Have you nothing better to do than to go around filming people when they're at their worst? I just lost my brother and his wife." People started walking away, but a few stayed. She turned to put on her shoe and leave when she saw her daughter coming down the street. "I'll get this finished up right now."

"Mother. The bank called and said you were trying to get into my accounts. I've told you before that's none of your business. Stay out of my information, or I'll have to have a restraining order put against you. I don't have time to keep running down here every time you get a burr up your ass about how much money I have in my accounts." She asked her how much she had in her accounts. "I'm not going to tell you. First of all, I'm a grown woman who makes her own money in life, and secondly, it's none of your business. I don't go around asking you how much money you have in your accounts, do I?"

"I'd tell you if you'd ask. I don't have any secrets to hide from you." She just looked at her, and

Debra had to turn away or feel guilty. She did have her secrets, and she wasn't going to be blabbing them to her just because she was pissed off. "Why are you keeping me from your accounts? I used to borrow from them all the time."

"Yes, and you'd make it so that I was short when it came time to cash checks for my rent and food. I don't like to have you running your nose in what I have in the bank. It's none of your business." She pointed out that she was her mother. "Yes, I understand that. You've always used that excuse when you want something that I have. Well, it's not going to work this time. I'm my own person, and you can't bully me into telling you. Because of you, I'm late going to the house to see what I want to keep or not."

"Don't keep any of it. I was just telling someone that Cindy had the worst taste when it came to decorating her home. The utmost worst." She told her that she always thought she had excellent taste. "You would. You just want to suck up to her. Well, it's too late for that now. She's dead, and good riddance to her."

"Mother! You don't mean that." She said that she did, and if she were here right now, she'd tell her to her face, too. "What did she ever do to you? Aunt Cindy was the nicest person in the world, next to Uncle Robert. I think they made a wonderful couple."

The smack to her face felt good, and Debra was drawing back to hit her again when she smacked her back. Holding her hand to her face, she asked her what she'd done that for and was told that she did it first. Well, that wasn't going to be all right with her.

"I'm your mother, and by rights I can hit you whenever I want." She was going to hit her in the face with her fist when Sen told her that she'd better be rethinking where her mind was going because she would give as good as she got. "We'll just have to see about that, won't we. And the next time you hit me, you'd better have a gun because I will. Do you understand me? I won't put up with you hurting your mother."

"He was right, you are dangerous." She didn't know who her daughter was talking about, but she was glad she was finally seeing her for what she was. Debra could be very dangerous when provoked. And right now her daughter was pushing all the right buttons to get herself killed. "Stay away from me, mother. I've had enough of you and the way you go around thinking that you can get away with anything."

"I will hang on to you until I get what I want, and if that means I'm going to get into your accounts, I will. You got more than I did, and I'm not happy. Don't you remember when you were a child, what happened to you when I wasn't happy? I miss those days." She could see fear on Sen's face and liked seeing it there. "You just give me what I want, and things will go well for you. However, if I find out that you've gotten more than me in my own brother's estate, I will kill you for it. I'm not kidding you right now."

"Stay away from me." When she turned her back on her to leave, Debra wanted to kick her down on the ground and beat her. But there were too many people around, and she didn't want to have to go back to jail. She remembered that as well. Ending up in jail wasn't anything that she wanted to happen again, either. Her brother had done that to her when she'd beaten Sen one afternoon. She remembered his words well. "You'll never see her again unless it's behind bars if you so much as slap her for doing something wrong." She said she was her kid. "For now, she is. I'm going to make arrangements to have her sent away to boarding school, and while she's there, you're going to get your shit together and remember why you have that nice house and car."

"You have nothing to do with either." Robert told her that he knew Howard. "Howard who? You think you know everything. Well, you don't. He wanted me to have this house."

"You blackmailed him. He gave you the house and the car for as long as you live so that you'd not tell people that he raped you. When we all know the truth, don't we, Debra? You got yourself pregnant with Sen and decided to blackmail the nicest man I've ever known. So you got a house and a car out of him in exchange, he's never to have anything to do with Sen. Christ, Sen would have been better off with Howard. But you couldn't just allow him to raise her, could you? You had to have something over him. Well, if you ever hit her again, I'll contact him and make sure he knows just what sort of mother you have been to his daughter. She's going to boarding school, and she'll love it. Anytime spent away from you is a good time, I'm sure of it."

That had been the last time they spoke, her and her brother. She was never invited to his home again, and when Sen came home from school, she would spend all her time with her uncle. Debra couldn't do shit about it because he had her in a place that wouldn't have boded well had she made a fuss. She liked living in the big fancy house with servants around all the time. She didn't have to do anything at all to stay there either. And you'd think that she was in heaven, but she wasn't.

The servants didn't answer to her. They kept the house cleaned up and the food cooked for her, but they didn't interact with her. She couldn't even fire them for not speaking to her, either. And they didn't unless she asked them a direct question about the household. The yard was mowed and trimmed along with the bushes. But as far as living in a great big house with all the servants, it was like living in a prison without anyone to talk to. She thought that was why she went to talk to her daughter so much. At least she would answer her questions when she had them.

She did wonder what ever happened to Howard Bash. He'd been a good time, but that had soured when she tried to get money from him about Sen. He was more than likely dead by now. Good riddens, she thought, and continued home. She was going to find out what happened to him, and then she was going to get more out of him. She needed to get what she wanted, and that was it.

Chapter 3

The house was perfect. She might get rid of a couple of things that weren't to her taste, but for the house, she was loving having so much space. Debra walked into the bedroom that her aunt and uncle shared and looked at all the boxes. She was donating their things, like clothing, to charity. There were other things like her uncle's collection of pocket watches that she was going to keep, as well as her aunt's jewelry collection that she remembered her wearing from time to time.

There were so many good and wonderful memories associated with the house. She remembered Christmases as well as other holidays. If it were something big, her aunt and uncle would celebrate it. Even Taco Day.

But it was the back end of the house that she was most amazed by. They had added rooms on, entire wings of rooms that would hold several families. There were six bedrooms with their own bathroom and kitchenettes. It looked as if they were planning to have people stay with them throughout the summer months as each room was decorated with a spring and summery theme. She did wonder if, at some point, it had been decorated for the holidays that just passed, but she wouldn't know since she couldn't ask them. It was things like that she would get the saddest about. Not being able to talk to them as they were no longer around.

It hurt her heart that she had lost them both at the same time. Of course, Aunt Cindy had died first in the accident, but that wasn't the same thing. They had died together, she supposed, like they would have wanted to, and that was good. But she missed them both so much it hurt her inside.

When the front doorbell rang, she went to answer it cautiously. She didn't want to encounter her mother today. Yesterday had been bad enough. Today, she wanted to bask in the love that was still around the house. The love that the two people she loved more than anyone else had shared with her. As she opened the door, she had a smile on her face, knowing that the man there wouldn't cause her any trouble at all. It was Ivan.

"I've come by to see if I could help any. The clinic is closed now, and I have all this free time." She said that she was just going through closets today and taking things out of them. "I can help lift them if necessary. I'm to understand that you've decided to donate everything that they wore. That's the best way to go. I can help."

"Great." She led him to one of the bedrooms and told him that everything in the closet had to go; he just had to make sure that he checked the pockets. "I've found all kinds of things in the pockets of my uncle's suits. Some money and some other items that he was fond of carrying, like chewing gum and toffee bits. I remember him always having some when I was a little girl and needing something to tide me over until lunch or dinner. He was a good man, and I'm going to miss him forever."

"I'm so sorry. I didn't have anyone in my life like that. My parents weren't the best people to be around." She said that she'd heard of them. "I don't know how you could live in this town and not have heard of them. They were the worst kind of people when we were growing up. My mother killed my father and blamed it on us so that we'd be sent to prison. That's where she is now. Life without parole."

"I'm glad that you guys were able to turn out so well. I've always heard that you are what you're made of, but I don't believe that. If I did, then I'd be a worse person than my mom. She raised me in my formative years. Then I was off to boarding school until I turned eighteen." He asked her if she'd had a good time there. "Yes. It was wonderful. I have so many friends that I can call on. I wouldn't, but I could." She smiled at him.

"I'll get started." He went into the bedroom that

held all her uncle's suits and ties. There were quite a few of them hanging in the closet that she wondered where he wore them all. She handed him a box that he could put the things he found in the pockets, and went to her aunt's closet. She had so many dresses with tags still on them, she wondered if she had a problem with shopping. Obviously, she could afford it.

She realized that she was hungry when Ivan said he'd gone through all the suits. They were laid out on the bed, and he was putting them in the tall boxes as he went. The box was full of candies and some money, and she had to laugh. Someone would have thought it was strange to get a suit with those things inside it.

Since there wasn't anything in the house they could eat, they decided to order out. There were a number of places that they could pick up from, but only a couple that would actually bring the food to you. So they settled on pizza again. It was that or subs, and that would have been too heavy for lunch.

Eating in the big kitchen, they decided that they had enough work done for the places that would pick up the things that she was donating. The boxes were in the living room now, and it would be easy for them to pick things up. She placed the call for the pickup, and they were on their way in a few minutes.

"What do you say to having dinner with me tonight?" She asked him if he was sure. "I am. I'd like to get to know you better, and I can't think of a way to do that other than us going out. It was so much fun the last time we went out with Devlin. Even though he did abandon us."

She said that she remembered. "It was nice, I will admit that. And I would like to get out of the house for a little while. It's been good getting things done around here, however. I do have to get the kitchen cleaned out. The things in the cabinet will be fine, but not the things in the refrigerator or the freezer. Luckily, they didn't have much in either one."

"I guess that would be because they had a cook. I've noticed that my brothers don't have much in the way of leftovers when they have a cook. I think the staff takes home what's left over." She said she didn't know she'd never had a cook or staff at all before. "Me either. I've only had someone come in and clean up after me once in a while. Like once a week, I guess. Other than that, I've never really had much in the way of help. But then I'm not really home all that much."

"I work a lot too. I clerk for Judge Rainer, and I love my job. He's the one who suggested that your brother go to the reading of the will with me. I'm ever so grateful that he did. I don't know what I would have done without him there." Ivan said his brother was handy for a lot of things that were law-related. "I guess so. I never wanted to be an attorney. I like what

I do, and that's about the extent of it."

"He works for my oldest brother and his wife most of the time. He does take on cases that he likes. And when he did that for you, I guess. He's a great brother. He also helped me out with the transfer of the vet's office to me. It wasn't that big of a deal, just an exchange of ownership, but it helped me from not having to find an attorney to do it for me." She said that it was nice having an attorney in the family. "It saves in having to find one that you can trust."

"I would imagine so. I trust the men and women I work for, but that's about all. They seem to do a good job when in the courtroom." She decided to change the subject and smiled at him. "This isn't talking about us. I was wondering how long you've been a vet? Not long, I'm guessing."

"About two years now. Only six months with my own. It's not been as hard starting out because everyone who was with the other vet just stayed with me. I had a built-in clientele. It made it nice because I could hit the ground running instead of trying to drum up business when I was just starting out. Doc Winter was a good vet, and people loved him. That's what I'm hoping for at the end of my career, someone to take over for me when I'm ready to retire."

"I never owned a pet in my life. Not even a goldfish. I was at boarding school when I was younger until I graduated from there. Then I went to college for a while and never had time for one there either." He said he thought every child should have a pet. "I'll maybe get one now that I have a house and yard. I noticed that the pool is fenced in, so I'd not have to worry about that. I might even just get me a cat to live indoors."

"We don't do well with cats being shifter wolves. Dogs are all right with us. With Lica being the alpha, they tend to hang around more when they're strays than not. You could get a kitten, and she could get used to me hanging around." She said she might do that. As a dog wasn't really her cup of tea. "You wound me."

They both laughed, and she made them a cup of tea each. She'd always loved the tea that her aunt would get for her, and she found the same brand and flavor in her cabinets. Making the cup for them both, they talked about what they enjoyed in food. She wasn't much of a taste tester when it came to new foods.

"I think it's the way that I grew up again. There wasn't much of a variety at school, and I guess I got used to that." He said that since he'd been out on his own, he'd been trying everything that he could get his teeth sunk into. "I'm going to have to get used to that, I guess. It might not be so bad as all that. I might find I like other foods."

"Good. We'll try that out tonight. You get something off the menu that you might not otherwise try, and we'll have fun trying each other's food. What do you say?" She laughed and told him that she'd give it a shot. "This will be fun for both of us, I think. We'll have some fun and find out if you like to branch out in different foods."

They talked about different foods that they ate, and she realized that she'd not eaten all that many different kinds when compared to him. He'd been trying foods since he'd been out on his own and could tolerate about anything, while she was picky about even what she had in her salad. She didn't care for cucumbers, and he loved them. Of course he did, she thought with a smile.

Once the fridge and freezer were cleaned up, she made a list of things that she would need if she were going to live here. She didn't see any reason why she wouldn't, but she was sort of afraid of her mother. If she found out anything about the money, she had a feeling that she would try to kill her. She was only just remembering when she'd been a child, and she'd beaten her so badly that she'd ended up in the hospital.

"I don't remember what had happened to cause her to beat me so badly. I do remember her hurting me severely. Uncle Robert made sure I was put in a nice room at the hospital. I was there for a couple of weeks." He asked what had been done to her. "I had stitches in my face and neck. Then I had a broken leg that I had to deal with when I was in the other school. They were good about getting me to classes, but other than that, I don't remember. Maybe I don't want to remember it was that bad."

"Could be. Some of the beatings that we got as kids, I remember well. But then there were others that would have put us in the hospital if we'd been able to go. My mother was more scary than my father. And he would egg her on about hurting us. I think that's why we were so afraid of her. She didn't know when to stop beating us when she started." Ivan told her of the time she'd beaten Edmond so badly with her high heel that he lost a toe. "He had to learn to walk without it, and that took him a long time. His wolf limps as well because of it."

"I'm sorry that you had to go through that. I can't imagine going through anything like that every day. Devlin told me once that the only time you got any relief from them was when they were in the jail system. And that wasn't often enough." He said they would get out and start on them that day. "I'm so very sorry you had that as a child growing up. As I said, I can't remember why my mother beat me, but I know that it was bad. So far as I know, it was only the one time, but you had it every day."

"We stuck together, the six of us. And when Mother went to prison, we stayed with the nicest couple around town to be raised by them until Devlin was old enough to leave home. And all we did was borrow enough money from them to buy our farm and work from there. I got to go to college because I worked hard and got good grades. It was hard for all of us to get an education, but we knew that we'd never make it in the world without one." She said that was why she'd gone to college, too. To better herself. "We have a lot in common, the two of us. That's good, don't you think?"

"I do. I think we'll get along well." Ivan left about four o'clock to go home and shower, and change. He said for her to dress up and they'd make an evening of it. She was looking forward to it as much as she was to anything else that she'd been doing of late and was glad that he'd asked her.

~*~

Ivan cleaned up his place a little bit before getting in the shower. He didn't have a huge mess, but he did have things lying around that should have been put away when he was finished with them. He did read his email about the houses that he was looking into. He wanted a house as much as his brothers did. After getting a shower, he decided that he'd look deeper into the email about the three houses and see what he could come up with. The other house was nice, but he thought that it had a lot of problems in the way it was laid out. There didn't seem to be much in the way of flow about the house, and that bothered him. But he'd stay if she loved the house. It was entirely up to her where they lived.

There were three houses that he liked, but one of them was well out of his price range. He really liked where it was sitting in relation to his brothers' homes, but it was a mammoth of a house with ten bedrooms and eleven baths. Filling it out would be expensive as well.

The other two houses were modest-sized homes. One of them had five bedrooms; one could be converted into an office. The other had four bedrooms but only one bathroom. He thought that would be a nightmare just waiting to happen if there were only one bathroom, so he decided to pass on that one.

Setting up a time to go and see the second house, he closed out his email and put his laptop away. He didn't have an office in the condo, but he did use the living room as much as he could when he had to be on the computer. It was nice in that he could watch television while he worked. Making fun of himself, he also had the biggest messes in the living room when he did that, too. Crumbs were everywhere, and he had two empty glasses in there as well. Cleaning up, he put everything in the dishwasher so that he could run it tomorrow. With just one person in the house, he didn't have to run it every day.

By the time he was ready to leave the house for dinner, he had cleaned up his house and made his bed with clean sheets. The washer had already done its part in cleaning his clothing and sheets, and he was just waiting for the dryer to finish its part. It would be nice to get into a nice, clean bed with clean sheets, and he found that he was looking forward to it almost as much as he was to his date.

Out the door on time, he started his car and made his way to Sen's house. She didn't live all that far away from him, but it was made a little more reckless by the streets being covered in snow from this morning. Spring was just a couple of weeks away, and he thought that it couldn't come soon enough for him. He was sick of the cold, wet snow and wanted the warmth of the sunshine to shine down on his poor old body. Laughing, he pulled into her driveway just as she was coming out with a bag in her hands.

"I didn't want to leave the trash in the house for tonight." He took it from her and put it in the trash cans that were at the end of the street. "I'm not sure what day they pick up around here, but since everyone else had theirs out, I thought that I'd do the same. It's going to be ugly tomorrow, isn't it?"

"We're not supposed to get any more snow tonight, but snow showers in the morning hours. I think that they'll call school simply because of the back roads that are around here." She said she agreed with him. "There are a lot of kids that live out in the boonies around here, and they have slick roads when the snow comes along."

"I never had that problem, so I don't know. I bet you did when you were growing up." He told her how he and his brothers all walked to school, so it was nice when school was called off because of the weather. "I guess I thought you were in the district that you'd catch a bus."

"If you lived within so many miles of the school, you had to walk. It made for a lot of walkers when I was in school." He took her keys from her to lock up the house. "I have made us some reservations at a nice place. I hope you don't mind."

"No, I'm excited about trying something different." They talked about how she was going to be venturesome tonight. "I think I'll have fun with you tonight. I've been looking forward to this all day. And you'll be happy to know that all the clothing has been picked up that was my aunts and uncles, so that's out of the way. Now all I have to do is figure out what I want to keep, which will be just about everything that's there, and do away with whatever I decide I don't need. I found a laundry room in the basement when I was looking around. I didn't even know there was one until then."

"I like that the house is all on one floor, but it doesn't flow all that well, does it?" She said that she'd noticed that today as well. That to get from one room to the next, you had to juggle your way around them. "I've lost my way to the bathroom a couple of times. It's a maze, I think."

"Yes, that's it. I was trying to think of what to call it, and you're absolutely right. It's a maze." She laughed. "I wonder how my family got around in the rooms when they were living here."

"Not easily, if I had to guess. Also, did you notice the kitchen? It's sort of laid out funny as well. Like it was a galley kitchen, and they turned it into what it is now. But it doesn't work all that well either. The stove is right next to the refrigerator, and when you open it, it is in front of the stove. That doesn't seem all that safe to me." She said she'd not noticed that until he mentioned it. "It's a lovely house, but it's laid out funny. And if you were to use the kitchen for all that long, say to make a large meal, it would really bother you in the way that things are laid out in it."

"I guess when I was looking around, all I could see was that I had a house. Now that you've pointed things out to me, I do wonder how they lived in it for as long as they did with all the problems. I noticed, too, that the addition is nice and smoothly laid out, but the connection between the addition and the house itself is way off." She thought about the rest of the house and shook her head. "I don't know now that I could live in the house the way it is. I'm glad you pointed things out for me. I would have noticed them after a while, but like I said, all I saw was that I had a house of my very own. I guess I should look into having it remodeled or buy something better. What do you think?"

"Maybe that's why they were forever having the house tinkered with. They were looking for a solution to the problem that we've noticed." She said she'd have to look around better when she got home. "But for now, we'll have a nice dinner and have a good time out. I love that they left you a house, however. It's really generous of them."

"I'm beginning to see lots of things that I didn't before. Not about the house, though that is one of them. I'm thinking about my mother and the fact that she and her brother never got along. I remember things from my childhood that didn't go over well with Uncle Robert. He would get into huge arguments with Mother and they'd not speak for weeks on end. Then, when she hit me, it was years. I don't know that they spoke at all when I was away at school. Do you suppose her hitting me had anything to do with that?"

"I would imagine, yes. He seemed to be pretty protective of you all the time. Then, when she did hit you that time, he sent you away so that you wouldn't be around her as much." She said that she also noticed that she'd not be home for the holidays, but at her uncle's house. "Could be that he figured that he paid for school, that you should be spending the holidays with him. That I can't help you with. I didn't know either one of them before they were killed."

"I'm remembering a lot more as time goes on. It's not like I tried to forget all the things that had gone on in my life, but things are starting to make sense now. Like, my mother is a bitch. I think I might have always known that, but she's always been about what I could give her. Even going so far as to take money from my accounts when I wasn't forthcoming about things that she wanted from me." She looked at Ivan and smiled. "We really are getting to know me in all this. How about you? I know you have a horrific childhood. Tell me when there were good times if you had any."

"I did when we were living with the Wilkins. They never treated us any differently than like we were their own children. I remember my first birthday with them watching over us. I had my first gift and cake. It was wonderful to be able to celebrate all our birthdays with them. They were the best couple that we'd ever had anything to do with." She asked him if he remembered what he'd gotten. "Yes, a sweater. Mrs. Wilkins had knitted each of us a new sweater for the colder weather. I think I might still have mine. I wore it all the time. It was such good memories to be able to look back over and remember. They were good to us. And for us too."

"It sounds like it. My mother was never about the holidays. I think she didn't like that she had to buy gifts for other people. She would just hand out cash when she got something from someone. I think she hated that as much as she did getting something for them. She's very selfish, I've only just noticed." He asked her if she'd ever figured out who her father was. "I know his name. It's on my birth certificate. Howard Bash. I remember that because there was a Howard at the parties that my uncle gave. I did wonder at one time if it was him or not, but I never asked. I wish I had now. I'd like to meet him."

"What would your mother say?" She told him she didn't know, but she'd more than likely be upset with her about it. "Did you ever ask her about your father? I mean, there has to be something out there about him, don't you think?"

"I think I will now that I'm older to see if she'll tell me anything about him. I deserve to know, don't you think?" He just smiled at her, and she grinned back. "Is that your way of telling me that I should do it even if it pisses my mom off?"

"It's up to you, but I know that I'd like to know more about the man who stayed out of my life since I was born. Even with his name on your birth certificate, it tells me that he was there during some point of your life that your mother felt comfortable enough with him to put his name there. Perhaps he's died or something, and she never wanted to talk about the love of her life. I don't know, but if you want to look for him, I know that Devlin can help you. He's pretty good at searching out things like that. For that matter, so are you. You have a name, the rest should be fairly easy."

"Knowing my mother, things will not be easy." He had to agree with her there. The little bit of time that he'd spent with her mother hadn't been good. She seemed to like it when things were full of drama, too. Something that he never cared for in all his life. He'd had too much of it as a child, he'd thought, and that was more than enough for him. He took her hand into his as they were being seated. "I'm excited to do this tonight. I love getting to know you. Or I guess you're getting to know me. I've been talking nonstop about myself. Tell me something about yourself, and let's talk about that."

Ivan talked about his adulthood, not his childhood. It was depressing to talk about when he was a child, and he thought that they could get more knowledge about each other if he stuck to his college years. And they had been fun. He'd met a lot of people then and had made a lot of friends. Then, when he graduated at the top of his class, he'd come back home to work with the vet who had wanted to retire. It was a good time for him, and he enjoyed telling her of some of the things that he'd gotten into as a teenager with his brothers. They had a wonderful dinner, and he hated to see it end.

"You really enjoyed the salmon?" She said it was wonderful and that she'd love to have it again. "I'm glad. It's one of my favorite all-time dishes. I can cook it at home too, but it's never the same. I keep trying, and maybe someday I'll get it, but for now I know where I can get a good dinner of it so that I can have it when I want it."

Chapter 4

Howard watched the young couple as they walked hand in hand down the little street. He'd been having someone watching over his daughter for years now, and this was the first time he'd seen her with a young man at her side, where she seemed to be enjoying herself. He knew about as much about the young man, Ivan Frazier, as he did himself. And all of it was good. He would enjoy talking to the man, but when the time was right. Howard kept an eye out for Debra so that she would not intrude on their time together.

He'd been blackmailed into leaving his daughter alone all these years. For as much as he wanted to be with her, there were his other children that he had to save as well. When Debra came to him to tell him that she was going to have his baby, he never believed her. It wasn't until she was born that he got the tests taken that proved without a doubt that she belonged to him that he started to take an interest in her. And he'd fallen in love with the child, too.

Howard had been divorced by then, his first wife having wanted to go and spend her golden years on spending money and having a good time. He'd just wanted to relax and have some downtime after working hard all his life, and they parted ways. The two of them had three children together, and they had grown up much like their mother. Flighty and spending money like they had an endless supply of it. He was glad when he married her that he'd had her sign a prenup, and that saved him from having to be broke all the time with the way that she spent money.

It was Debra's plan all along to ruin him by telling people that he was a pedophile. Not that it mattered to him all that much, but it would have ruined his chances with his children. They would have grown up with the thought that he had done things to them that a father shouldn't, and he didn't want to give them that out. They would have used it too, to make it so that he had to pay them more money. He knew that without a doubt. They were as greedy as their mother had been, and, as it turned out, as greedy as Debra had been too. Thankfully, it had only cost him a house payment once a month and money in her account. Not as much as she wanted, but enough to keep her happy with her lot in life and to leave him alone. He thought that he made out better than she did as he got to see his daughter grow up without Debra being any the wiser.

If not for Robert and Cindy Ranger, he might not have been able to spend as much time with his daughter as he liked. They would have her home for holidays and summer vacations, and he'd be there as much as he could. He'd also been able to pay for her boarding school, then her higher education when the time came. Howard had put a lot of time and effort into being there for his daughter when she needed him, and now that Robert and his lovely wife were gone, he was going to have to contact her after all these years. He was both nervous and excited about the prospect of meeting her face to face with her knowing that she was his daughter.

"Mr. Bash, there's a phone call for you on line two. She said that she has information about your daughter." He asked if there was a name. "She didn't give one. I did ask, but she kept changing the subject around so that I wouldn't get it. She's very slick, I will admit that."

"Hello?" He waited on the line for a few seconds before he repeated his greeting and said his name. "I'm Howard Bash. You wanted to speak to me?"

"Yes. I'm sorry. I didn't hear you come back on the line. My name is Brandy Fraizer. It's amazing what you can find out when you have a seemingly endless supply of money. Of course, it helped that I had your name. I'm the sister-in-law to your daughter, Serenity Ranger Frazier." He stood up, then sat down twice more before he found his tongue. "I'm guessing that you didn't expect someone to find you. You didn't make it hard, I will say that for you. Debra is giving her a hard time again, and I thought you'd like to know that she's getting married soon. Not Debra, but your daughter, Sen."

"I didn't know she was dating that man, and it was serious." She told him how they were mates and that Ivan would make sure she was safe as he could, but it was Debra who was causing them the most trouble. "How can I help? I was just thinking that I need to talk to Serenity. Robert was my go-between for us. I don't think she'd remember me all that much if not for them."

"As you've no doubt heard, they're both gone. Car accident. Sen is living in their house for now. When I spoke to them yesterday, they were house hunting. Something about the house being too much of a maze for them to be living in it. They've decided to find them something that they both can enjoy." He asked her if it had to do with the kitchen. "I'm not sure, but if that's the first thing that you think of, then that's more than likely a big part of it. The two of them are getting along very well, but as I said, for her mother. She's not a nice person, is she?"

"No, she's not. I've been dealing with her for the past twenty-four years, and it's never gotten any better with her. She's going to have to stand on her own two feet here in a few months when Serenity turns twenty-five. I no longer have to support her." She asked if he was paying for the big house she was living in. "You know a great deal about me when I don't even remember your name. You said it was Frazier. The only Frazier that I know is the owner of a large slaughterhouse that just went up. He's doing well, too, if my sources are correct."

"I'm married to him. Lica Fraizer. Sen is going to be marrying his brother Ivan. Ivan is a vet of good standing." He started taking notes on the conversation so that he could go over it later. He would have to do a search of his own before the end of the day. "I'm arranging a little get-together that I'd like for you to attend. Sen will be there. She knows that I'm trying to reach you. As I said before, you've made it easy to find you. Was that on purpose? So that she could find you if she wanted?"

"That's right. I wanted her to be able to find me if she ever needed me. I've waited a long time now, and I'm guessing that it's taken her so long because of her mother." She said that some of it had to do with her. The other was that she didn't have the funds. "I didn't give her all the money that I could have because I didn't want to make Debra any more pissed off than she usually is. She hates that people have more than she does at any given time, and I didn't want my daughter hurt again."

"She's putting together pieces of her childhood from memories now. She said that she had such a wonderful childhood that the only thing she could attribute it to was having her aunt and uncle in the picture. I have a feeling that you were the one who was footing the bills when it came to Sen." Howard told her that she was right. But they did make it so that he could see her when she came to the house for events. "I figured as much. You did well, Howard. She thought that the man named Howard was her father, but she was never for sure about it. I'm glad you didn't just let her be raised by that psychopath of a mother."

"Has she threatened her again?" She told him of the details of the death of her uncle and aunt, and how she was a billionaire. And that Debra threatened to kill her if she got more than she did from the estate. "That sounds like her. She only hit her the one time that I'm aware of, and I took her from her mother. Debra was never stable about things when it came to money. She was forever trying to get more out of me since Serenity was just a baby. But as I said, when Serenity turns twenty-five, everything stops for her mother, and the house that she's living in will revert to my child. There will be no more money put into her account, nor will the house be hers to live in as she sees fit. Everything that I own will go to Serenity when I pass away, too. My other three children are on their own when it comes to living in this world."

"Is that someone else she's going to have to deal with when you pass away? Your other children? If so, you'd better be doing something about them now. I don't have much tolerance for people who try to hurt what I consider my family, and Sen is the moment she became Ivan's mate." He said that he'd dealt with them and they know better now. "I hope you're right. I would hate to have to take you to task if one of them gets out of hand. I'm not without a great deal of resources myself."

He didn't know what she'd do to him once he was dead, but he had a fear of her all the same. Telling her again that his children had been dealt with had her telling him he'd better didn't bode well for him. Howard decided that he was going to have another talk with his children to make sure they understood that he was finished with them. So far, they seemed to understand, but he was going to make his point again. There was no point in pissing anyone off after he was dead. He had a feeling that she'd be digging him up and causing him all kinds of trouble if things went south with his kids. She was sort of scary.

After getting the information that he needed about the event that he'd get to formally meet his little girl, he got the caller's name again. She told him that, as well as her social security number, so that he could do a very detailed background check on her. Yes, he thought, she was scary as fuck, and he wasn't going to mess with her if he didn't have to. But to see his daughter again and letting her know how he was related to her, was going to be wonderful.

When they rang off, he thought about the dinner party that he was going to. Brandy had told him that it would be a casual affair and that he didn't need to wear a suit. That the other men would be in jeans and shirts. He said that he owned some blue jeans and would feel comfortable wearing them as well. As soon as he wrote the date on his calendar, he had his secretary clear the whole day for him, knowing that he'd get nothing done that day because of the anticipation of getting to know his daughter more.

He didn't get much done today, either, he realized at five o'clock. He'd had his computer go to sleep so many times that he gave up trying to make it work for him. As he was putting his things away, he always liked a clean desk first thing in the morning, and he thought about things that he hadn't in some time. Mostly, it had to do with Debra and her antics. But he also thought of the first time he'd met her. She'd been such a beauty that she took his breath away. It was sad to him that the inner shell of her had been so rotten.

They'd been at a party. He'd only decided at

the last minute to go to the thing, as he had better things to do than to go to an event that had to do with an engagement of one of his friends. The couple had thrown a large launch party, they called it, and they wanted all their friends to get to know the future missus, whatever their names had been at the time.

Debra had cornered him in an empty room, and they'd had sex on their first meeting. He knew better, but he'd been so infatuated that he'd let things slip up, and he'd ended up with Serenity. Not that he minded. He'd been divorced by then, and things were looking dim on the family front that he welcomed a child — so long as it was his — that he could raise with someone. Turns out that Debra had her own plans, and they didn't include him in her party of two, and she blackmailed him when he had insisted that he have a part in raising his daughter, too. The thing that had always bothered him was that everything she wanted from him was for her and not the child. She never asked for support or any of the other things that went with having a child. He had a feeling that the child had been a ploy to get money from him, and he fell for it. Well, he got a child out of it, too. Debra just didn't know anything about his involvement in her life.

Then she'd beaten the child. When Serenity had been six years old, she'd been beaten by Debra so badly that she had to stay a week and a half in the hospital.

Her leg had been broken, and her wrist sprained. There were stitches, too, that had to heal, and he never forgave her for that. The next thing he did was have her sent to a school far from Debra, and she seemed to be all right with it. He would never forgive her for beating a helpless child the way that she had, and he planned on telling her when the time came. Just a short few months, and he'd have everything just where he wanted it. Debra out of his life and his daughter in his.

~*~

"And he wants to meet me?" Brandy told her that she'd already met him as he was a guest at her aunt and uncle's home all those times she'd been there. "I thought as much. I never asked because no one said anything. I'm assuming that there was some kind of law my mother made up that he wasn't allowed to see me."

"He had to stay out of your life until you were twenty-five, or if you wanted to meet him. I made it clear that you were having me look for him, and he seemed excited about getting to know you. I found out from his lawyer, who contacted me a couple of days later, that he's paying for the house that your mother has been living in for so long as she doesn't cause any trouble for him. Also, he pays the taxes and has the house renovated every five years by having the walls painted and the carpets replaced if they need it. Needless to say, she has nothing to do with the renovations other than to be out of the house when they're going on. Could be when she was trying to live with you all those times." Sen said she could think of times when she had no place to live too. "I have the contract that was made up about you being his child. Everything that your mother gets right now will stop when you turn twenty-five. On the day of your birthday, she will be removed from the house, and all money will stop being put in her account. If you had thought to get in touch with him sooner, it would have stopped then. I think this is great. He's a smart man for wanting to have it in the contract that she can not harm you in any way. I think that's when you were shipped off to boarding school so that she couldn't hurt you anymore."

"That's what Ivan and I thought." Brandy handed her the contract, and she handed it to Devlin. He'd come to their home to see what her dad had to say about meeting her, and she was overwhelmed at the information that she was getting. "He's wealthy then, I take it."

"Very much so. About as wealthy as we are as a family. He's got a good head on his shoulders about investments and the company that he owns, which sells high-end furniture all over the world and does a good job of it. He has houses everywhere that are good vacation spots, and he rents them out to people with too much money on their hands. Like I said, a smart businessman." She asked about his life. "I have a lot of information about his life before you came into the picture. He has three children from his wife, and they divorced about five years before you were born. Howard is a young man considering what he's done with his life, and I like what I've read about him. His kids are shits, but they have nothing to do with him or his money. He keeps them at arm's length away from him, and his ex-wife is out of the picture completely. She has her own life and never seems to bother with her kids either."

"He sounds like he might be lonely." Brandy told her that he has a very lively social life and he stays on top of his own investments. He is a hard worker and a good friend to those who think to call him such. "He and my uncle were good friends then. I guess I kind of figured that out on my own."

"Howard was his best man when he married Cindy. They would go on vacations together, just the two men, and would go on hunting trips too. Cindy never got along with his ex-wife, so she was never one to go on vacation trips with them." She asked how she'd gotten so much information with only a phone call. "The attorney for his personal life called me, like I said. He was very forthcoming and told me everything that he knew. I guess he figured that since you wanted to meet him, then you should know everything there was to know about him. Also, you should know that you're named in his will in the event that anything happens to him. That will make you a very wealthy woman."

"I'm not concerned with the money." Brandy said that she'd figured that she'd say that. "I have enough money now to do with what I want. I'd rather have a relationship with him than have him die on me, too. I can't wait until this dinner thing. I can't thank you enough for setting it up for us. I kind of hope that my mother finds out that I'm seeing him so that she can get pissed off enough to leave me alone."

"Do you think she will do that?" Sen had to think about it for a few minutes and realized that Brandy was right in asking. No, she wouldn't be all right with her contacting her father. "We'll just make sure to keep things quiet while we're waiting for you to see him. After that, you know that this entire family will protect you. Ivan or any of the men will die for you."

"I know they keep saying that, but it's hard for me to believe that they'd do that for a stranger. Ivan and I are just getting to the point where he kisses me goodnight. I can't imagine him dying for me. I don't even want to think about that." Brandy said she understood. "Good. I've decided that I'm terrified of what my mother will do to me when she finds out about the money. I'm even more afraid of her if she finds out about my dad. She'll try to hurt all of us. Dad included."

"She's not stable, I was told. That might be something that you keep in mind while talking to her. She might lash out at you or do something that will harm you in a big way. I'd not put anything past her." She said she'd be careful of her. "Good. I don't think that I'd go out alone anymore either. You don't want her catching you off guard at any point, or she might hurt you badly. From what the attorney said about her, she's being watched all the time when you're around, just so that she doesn't harm you again. Do you know why she did so in the first place?"

"I don't. I tried to remember, but I can only remember the pain of it all. Then, afterwards, being shipped off to boarding school right away." Brandy told her. "All I did was ask after my father, and that had her losing control? Why? It seems like a perfectly good question for a kid to ask about someone that's not in the picture."

"She would lose it all if you were to ask about your father, remember? She had to keep you from asking so that she'd be able to keep her money and house. With you being curious, that would have ended it all." She said she never knew that as a child. "Even as an adult, she had to make sure that you never tried to find him. I think that's what had her hating you being around your uncle and aunt, they knew your father from before you were born."

"I guess my life is a bit more complicated than I thought it was. All this mystery about my childhood could have been so dangerous. I guess it was." She thought about her mother and wondered what she would do if she knew that she was going to see her father in a few days. She'd have a fit that was for sure. And would more than likely hurt her again for doing it. "I hate that she has this hold over me. Like I'm some sort of child that needs to be kept in the dark about their father. It's not like he's a monster or anything. Even though, come to find out, she is. I always knew there was something off about her. I just never realized how extensive it was."

They talked about the dinner and what kind of food they'd be having. Brandy thought it was wonderful that Howard's attorney had sent over a list of things that he couldn't eat. He wanted to be a part of this family so badly that he'd opened up his entire life to them and didn't hold back on answers.

"I was told that if you thought of something else you wanted to know, you were to call the office. You might not get to talk to the attorney when you did, but Howard would always take your call, no matter what."

She thought that was very sweet and said as much. "He really wants this to work. I've never known someone to be so open with their lives before. I don't even get this much information when I'm doing a merger for a company."

"What have you told him about me?" Brandy said there wasn't much he didn't already know about her. "So he's been keeping tabs on me my entire life. I guess that's not creepy or anything." They all laughed. "I don't know what to think about this right now. I'm excited but nervous too. I can't wait to see him again. It's been a long time in coming, don't you think?"

"I think this is a man who has been waiting his entire life for you to come into it and has had the first bit of good news since then. His friendship with the Rangers has been a long one, and I'm betting if asked, he knows what kind of grades you made in school, as well as has every school picture ever taken of you. He would have been right on top of everything having to do with you." She thanked Ivan for his kind words and laid her head on his shoulder. "He, like me, has been waiting for you all this time and now has the opportunity to be with you. Just like I have been."

For the rest of the evening, they talked about the slaughterhouse. It was coming along nicely, and they'd been able to sell their beef to local stores that needed it. They'd only been open for a short time and were already having people come back to get more of their beef so that they could stock their freezers. She loved that they all worked for the place, with the exception of Ayden.

Ayden had been working for Brandy to go to places to see why they were losing money. Once, he'd been working as a dishwasher at a high-end restaurant, and they were losing money. Come to find out they were selling off the meat that was to be used at the restaurant and selling human flesh to the customers, the employees. Ayden had been eating at the place for over a week by then and had gotten an aversion to red meat after finding that out. Not only him, but his wolf as well, couldn't stand to be around it or even to smell it on someone else's plate, or he'd be sick. She felt sorry for him and was glad that the people at the restaurant had all been arrested.

By the time dessert was being served, she was full. They always had good dinners when they went to Brandy and Lica's home, and this was no exception. The pork chops had been braised in something peppery, and the au gratin potatoes had been her favorite. She ate a little pie but was too full to eat much more than a couple of bites of it.

"I had the strangest animal in today. Usually, I get in dogs and cats with an occasional hamster. But today I was to see an emu. I only had to make sure that they were healthy, as I don't know exotic animals all that well, but it was odd having one in the office." Lica said he'd never seen an emu before. "Me either, but in the zoo. But the woman who brought him in said that she raises them, and this one had been acting off. As I said, I don't specialize in exotic animals, and she had to take him to Columbus, but it was something that I'm going to remember from now on."

"How is your business going, Ivan? I've not heard that you were having any troubles. I guess you did all right by buying up old man Wiggins' place." He said that he was having fun and he thought that was the best part of his job. "Good. I noticed, too, that you've put in for a couple of shifts at the slaughterhouse. Just don't overdo it. We have enough people working for us now that we don't have to come in to cover anymore. Just remember that when you're too tired. We're doing all right now."

"I will, but it gets me out of the house." Lica told him that he knew how that was. "Sometimes it's just good to see something different. I get to talk to the others, too, when I'm there. That's a rare treat for me when everyone is so busy all the time. I usually can't wait until we have our Thursday dinners. It's the highlight of my weeks."

Sen knew that the men all got together once a week, and the women in the family did as well. They never talked of business when they were out with each other, and that was good. It was their time to catch up on their daily lives and get to know what was going on. Even with the new baby in the family, there was much to talk about, and she was looking forward to her first dinner with the women. She liked them all very much.

After dinner, she and Ivan went back to her place. The more time she spent in the place, the more she could find wrong with it. While she was happy to have a house, this one wasn't one that she wanted to make her forever home. Tomorrow, she and Ivan were going to look at a couple of houses around town and see what they could find. She also wanted to get to know him a little better. They were having so much fun just talking that she sometimes forgot that they hadn't known each other all that long. It seemed like he'd been in her life forever.

She wondered what he'd say if she told him that she was falling in love with him. Ivan was the kindest person she'd ever met, and she loved to watch him with the animals that he worked with. Sometimes she'd just go sit in his waiting room to meet the animals that he treated. He thought she was silly, but she didn't care. She thought it was great that animals trusted him so much when they didn't feel well or were hurt.

Chapter 5

Debra didn't want to meet her daughter for lunch unless she got to pick out the place. It would be someplace cheap, and she didn't care for that when someone else was paying. She'd better have her banking information on her so that she could get into her accounts again. This was just bullshit that she was blocking her from her money when she wanted some of it. As soon as she showed up at the place, she knew two things at once.

There was a man with Sen, and the place was simply too cheap for her to even show her face at. They served things like burgers and salads. She wanted to have steak and potatoes for her lunch, and Sen knew it. She didn't sit down but told the man that he had to leave.

"He's the reason that I wanted to meet you today. We're getting married." It was a good thing there was a chair behind her, or she might have ended up on her ass. Sitting there staring at her daughter, she couldn't believe that after all this time, she was throwing something like that at her. "Mother? Don't you have something to say?"

"I do. I forbid you to get married. You're too

young, and I won't have it." Sen just laughed. It wasn't like her to be laughing when she put down the law. "You heard what I said. Now get rid of him so that we can talk about business. And there will be no more conversations about marriage. I don't want to be known as old enough to have a married daughter."

"I'm almost twenty-five, Mother, and I'm well old enough to be getting married. And frankly, I don't care what your opinion is about it; he's asked me, and I said yes. The only reason that we're doing this the way that we are is that I didn't want you to be able to make a scene." Debra looked around and decided that she was going to do just that. Make a scene so that the young man would be too embarrassed to be seen with either one of them again. "You make a scene right now, and I'll walk out of this restaurant, and you'll be here all alone. I don't care what you have to say about us getting married. The only reason we're here is so that you didn't find out when you read it in the newspaper."

"Like I care what people think." She decided that she was going to scream and took in a deep breath to do so. When the man put his hand over hers, she nearly did scream when it morphed into a great paw. "What sort of monster do you think you're marrying? He's got a paw as a hand, Sen. What do you have to say about that?"

"He's a shifter wolf." When the man came to take their order, she was too mesmerized by the paw to make any kind of order in her head. Someone must have ordered for her because when the paw disappeared into a hand, the waiter was gone. She looked at Sen. "Your mouth is hanging open. People are beginning to stare at you."

Snapping her mouth closed, she looked around the room. People were indeed staring, and she hated that. If the attention was going to be on her, she wanted to be the one in control of it. And she wanted to be the one who had started it. Picking up her napkin, she noticed that she had a small cut on her hand. Licking the blood off, she heard the man laugh.

"I have a connection with you now." She didn't know if that meant anything to her, but she was suddenly afraid. Shifters were all monsters, and she didn't want anything to do with them. This man was a wolf, and she knew that he was more than likely some kind of dog monster. "You might want to know, too, that I can read your mind. There isn't much in there, but enough for me to know that you might want to be looking for yourself another home."

"Why? What do you know?" It was Sen who answered her, and she didn't like that any better. "What do you know of you turning twenty-five? You stay out of my business. You'd better not be talking to your father. So help me, I'll kill you if you have been."

"As a matter of fact, I have been. You told me nothing about him, so I thought I'd look and see what I could find out on my own." She slapped her hand down on the table and told her to stop that right now. "I'm afraid it's too late. I've dinner plans with him tonight, and we're going to get to know one another."

"I forbid it." Sen laughed again. "I don't think this is the least bit funny, Sen. The man wanted nothing to do with you, and my word should be enough. I demand that you stop this nonsense right now and forget about seeing him. He's nothing to you."

"But my father. Right? I mean, you put it right there on my birth certificate, what his name is. All I had to do was request a copy of it to get married, and there it was. He was easy enough to find, too. It wasn't as if he was trying to hide from me. And once I spoke to him, he told me all kinds of things that I didn't know before. Like you blackmailed him to stay out of my life. I might not have believed it, but he has the contract that you signed when you had him staying away." Debra was dizzy with anger, and she might well have slapped her daughter but for the man sitting next to her. He was looking at her as if he knew what she was planning.

"You touch her, and I'll kill you by ripping your throat out right here at this table. I'm not messing around with you today. You so much as pull your hand back to do her harm, and that will be the end of you." She shivered, knowing on some level that he wasn't kidding about what he'd do to her either. "Here comes your food. Eat it and keep your mouth shut. Or I will shut it for you. As I said, I'm in no mood to mess with you."

"Do you hear the way that he's talking to me? Have you no say in what he's threatening to do to me?" Sen said that she was on the same page as he was. "You're going to side with him after everything I've done for you?"

"What is it that you've done for me, Mother? Nothing if you're going to be thinking on that. You've done nothing but keep me from a father that I'm looking forward to being around. A good deal more so than I want to be around you." She picked up her burger and bit down into it. "This is really good. You should enjoy it before we leave."

"Where do you think you're going?" Before she could think about what she was doing, Debra picked up her sandwich and took a bite of it. It was her favorite, ham and Swiss cheese. Just the way that she liked it. With the crunchy toast and the slices of ham so thin that she could read through them. But she'd never tell Sen that. Or the man next to her. But she had a feeling that he knew. He seemed to know everything that was going on. "I asked you a question. Where is it that you think you're going? We're not finished with this conversation yet. You'll not be seeing your father, and you'll not be getting married. That's final. What I say goes with you, Sen, or so help me I'll kill you when I find out where you're meeting him. Him too for being a bastard all my life."

"You mean providing you with a house and car? Money each month when you needed it? Is that what you consider treating you poorly? If only I had known that you had money at your disposal, I wouldn't have taken you out to lunch at all, with you telling me you nearly broke me when I needed the money more than you did." She took another bite of her burger and smiled at her. "But I'm not worried about you any longer. When I get married, which is going to happen and soon, I'll be living a grand life with Ivan here, and we'll not think of you at all. I wish there were a reason I could send you off to prison, that would just make my day. But I can't, so I guess I'll have to put up with you the old-fashioned way and avoid you at all costs. Which won't be hard, I don't think. You won't have any place to live once I meet with my dad tonight. That was the stipulation, right? Once I met him on my terms, your contract with him is null and void."

"Why are you treating me this way? I've done nothing wrong to you. You've lived a good life thanks to me." She asked her if she meant being sent to a boarding school. "I made that happen for you."

"By beating me because I asked about my father? Yes, I remember that. You nearly killed me when I asked you where he was." She said she got to live, didn't she? "Yes, no thanks to you. I was rushed away from you and spent some wonderful years with my aunt and uncle. I know, he's your brother. But he loved me. You? I'm not so sure."

"Howard was a monster. Did he tell you that he was a pedophile? I bet that never came up when he was telling you all about himself." She said that it didn't because it wasn't true. "So you believe him over me?"

"Yes. Any day of the week." That hurt, and she wasn't sure why. She wanted this meeting to go her way, and she wasn't sure how to get it back under her control. Even if she ever had it. "You think about all the things that you're going to be missing when he pulls the rug out from under you in a few days. For all I know, he might well have started it already."

"You think you're so smart. Well, we'll see what happens when he tries this shit on me. I'll have him in court so fast that his head will spin. Then we'll see what a great father he is to you." She told her that didn't make any sense. "Yes, it does. You're just looking for excuses to try to make me look bad. For all you know,

I'm the one who has been keeping you safe from him all these years. Did you ever think of that?"

"The only time I think of you is when I think that you're going to try and hurt me. And usually that's daily. I'm sick of running my life with the thoughts of what you'll do to me if you find out. There are lots of things that I keep from you so that you don't try to hurt me. But that time is over. I'm going to be my own person from now on and not have another thing to do with you." She told her she was just showing off in front of the man. "Am I? How would you know anything about me, Mother? I mean, you've barely spent five hours with me at any one given time, and that was when you were bitching about what I wasn't giving you. Or doing for you. As I said, I'm finished with you and all your threats."

"You'll be sorry about this, Sen. I swear to you I'm going to hunt you down sometime soon and make sure you understand that you don't want to fuck with me." She said she was finished with her, so it didn't matter. "We'll see about that. I'm a lot more dangerous than you think. You've messed with the wrong person."

"We'll see, as you're so fond of saying. I'm not worried about you. If you try to come at me, I'll have you arrested so fast...how did you put it? Oh yeah, your head will spin." Laughter from the two of them had her blinded by the anger that she was feeling.

"Mother, you might want to remember something else. I know all about you, and you know very little about me. I might have found that sad to know, but I'm glad for it now. You won't be able to get past my new family, and that's a promise."

When the two of them stood up, she did as well. While she was still pissed off at the two of them, she also knew that there would be a time when she'd get to Sen. And when she did, she was going to make the last time she hurt her look like an easy day in the park. She was just mad enough to kill her this time, and she would if she could, too.

Outside in the sunshine, all she could think about was how badly her head hurt. Anger would do that to her until she found an outlet. It would make her sick to her stomach, too, if she didn't find an outlet soon. Stomping her way to her car, she was nearly blinded by rage and walked by where she had parked her car twice before she realized it was gone.

She might well have parked it in the wrong spot, so she went through the parking lot three times to try to find it. As she was walking past the places where she could have parked it, she saw Howard Bash across the street.

He waved at her, and before she could think about what she was doing, like a fool, she waved back at him. While she couldn't hear his laughter from where she was, she could see that he was getting a jolly good laugh about her from where he was. Damn it all to fuck and back, he was doing what he'd said he would. Leaving her homeless and without a car.

Hurrying back to her house, she was just getting there as the police and locksmith were leaving. The locks would be changed, and everything that she owned was still inside. Not like she had any money stashed away. As soon as she got her money monthly, she'd spend it. It was why she would try to get a meal or two out of Sen; she'd be broke within a couple of weeks of getting paid. Ten grand didn't go as far as it used to, she knew this. Since she didn't have any bills to pay, not a single one, she'd spend her money on whatever she wanted and damn being broke in a few weeks. Now all that was gone, and she had no one to blame but her daughter.

"The bitch will pay for this." Debra knew that she'd only had a few months until she turned twenty-five, and she would have lost it anyway. But she was counting on Howard not knowing the date of his daughter's birthday and giving her some extra time. Not that she'd have been any more prepared for it than she was now. But she might well have been, she told herself.

She didn't know what she was going to do now. She'd never been one to save any money for later. And now that things were going to be gone from her usage, she was going to have to figure out a way to get some more money. She wished now that she had not spent all the money from her brother's estate. That might well have come in handy about now.

"There has to be more money than I got." There was no way that her brother only had what she'd been given. The house that Sen got was all right at first, but now that she didn't have any place to live, she might well have to make amends and live with her for a while. She had the room; it was a two-bedroom home, wasn't it? "Damn it, I wish I had been around my brother more when he was alive. I might have gotten more money."

Water under the bridge, as the old saying went. She was out of a home and car, and money. Her next check wasn't coming, so she wasn't going to be able to afford to get another place to live without money. This was all Sen's fault, and the sooner she could find her, the better, so that she could kill her. Whatever was hers was going to be Debra's as soon as she was dead, and that was suiting her just fine. She only had to figure out how to get her alone before she could get rid of her for good.

~*~

Ivan understood the reason for the lunch date. He didn't like it, but he understood that getting Debra out of the house was the way that Howard could have the locks changed. Since the house was in his name, he could do whatever he wanted to it. The car being repossessed was the next thing that he'd done. All of it was going to cause trouble for Sen, and he wasn't going to be happy if something happened to her in the process.

"I swear to you that she's going to be fine. I have someone watching Debra all the time, and if she comes within a few feet of her, they'll take her down." That all sounded good, but a lot could be done within a few feet, especially if the other person had a gun. Ivan didn't like this at all. Not one bit. "You have to trust me."

"I don't actually. And I don't trust Debra either." Howard told him that he didn't either. "Good, then we can be on the same page about her. She's going to be dead if she tries to hurt Sen, and I'm not going to be happy with you either. She's dangerous, and she'll stop at nothing to get what she feels is coming to her."

"I understand." Ivan didn't think that the man did, but said nothing more. He was going to have to quit his job if things continued on the way that they were, and he was going to blame that on Howard. The man thought that he was smarter than Debra. Perhaps so, but she was still more dangerous than he was. Any day of the week. "I promise you nothing will happen to Serenity as long as I have breath in my body."

"If something does happen to her, you're not going to be worrying about getting to be an old man; I'll rip your throat out where you stand. I'm not one to fuck with either, and she's my mate. I will die trying to protect her." Howard said that he felt the same way about her. "I doubt very much that will mean much when you're dead. Debra will go after you, too. And whichever one of you she gets to first will be dead. She won't care who it is."

He could tell that Sen was worried now that she'd thought about it. This morning, it had been a lark, something that she could do to her mother to get back at her. But in the cold light of the day, it was telling her that she'd made a mistake and that Debra was going to come after her. Ivan told her to stick with him, and he'd protect her, but he could only be in one place at a time. Like he thought to himself earlier. He was going to have to quit his job in order to protect Sen.

"I wanted to tell you something." He nodded, pushing the hair that was over her forehead out of the way. "I've fallen in love with you. I didn't know it was possible after us only knowing each other for so little time, but it's the best feeling that I've ever had in my life. I feel like I could take on the world and come out on top. I'm so in love with you."

"I have wanted to tell you that I love you for

weeks. I think I fell in love with you that first night I saw you with my brother." She kissed him on the cheek. "Surely we can do better than that. We just professed our love for each other. I would love a real kiss."

He pulled her into his arms and held her close. Looking down at her, he knew on all kinds of levels that he'd never love anyone like he did her. She was the one and only for him, and he couldn't have been happier. He told her that he loved her again and pulled her in for a kiss that would bring them together.

Tasting her, he was thrilled at how much she was giving him. Ivan had kissed women before, but there was no comparison to the kiss he was getting from Sen. She tasted of the honey that she'd had in her tea. Fresh flowers were the scent that he could smell when he was near her. Everything about this woman brought him happiness, and he couldn't have let her go right now if his life depended on it. He was in love for the first and only time in his life.

When they finished with the kiss, he held her to his body. He knew that she could feel his erection, and there wasn't anything that he could do about it. When she moved her hips closer to his, he moaned at the feeling and kissed her again. This time, he didn't hold his passion in check but loved the way that she responded to him. It was like having a bit of heaven with her in his arms.

"If we keep this up, we'll never make it home but might be arrested for having sex right here on the sidewalk." She giggled, and he laughed. It was a wonderful sound to hear her giggle, and he would love to hear it more often. "I'm supposing that I should take you home before things get out of hand. We only have a few days, and we'll be married at the courthouse. Are you sure you're all right with that?"

"I don't know that I'd be able to stand waiting for a big wedding to happen. I want to be your wife now." She looked up at him and smiled. "Besides, the sooner we get this over with, the better. I want to be your wife in the worst sort of way. To be called Serenity Fraizer is the best thing that will ever happen to me."

"I agree. I can't wait to introduce you as my wife. I already do that now, but to make it official will be great." He pulled away from her, sure that he was going to do as he said and make love to her right on the sidewalk. There would be much for people to talk about, but he didn't care. She'd be his, and that was what he wanted. But in a more quiet setting. At least more private anyway. "We should get home. We have those houses to look at tomorrow morning, and that will take up most of our day. I'll go home to my lonely bed, and you'll get to sleep in your big bed alone too."

"You're silly." Walking hand in hand to his car, he held the door open for her when she got in. Once he was in the car and buckled, he turned to her and kissed her on the cheek. "We'll have to make plans to make love soon. I want you so badly now that I ache from it."

"I do you as well. But we need a place to be able to have some privacy, and house hunting won't give us that." She asked him about tonight. "You want me to spend the night with you? That would be fantastic. And fun. If you're sure. I don't want to rush you into anything that you're not willing to do."

"You didn't suggest it, I did." She smiled at him. "Yes, I want you to come and sleep with me. And to have sex. I want you, as I said."

"All right. We'll go to my place as it's got clean sheets on the bed. I want you to know that I've never taken anyone back to my place before." She said that she was glad that he'd said that. "You'll get more magic. I'm not sure how that will affect you when you do get it. Brandy and the others were down for a few hours when they got it, so I want you to remember that. Are you sure you want to do this?"

"I'm about as sure of it as I have been anything in my life." She looked out the front window of his car and smiled. "We'll never get there if we don't leave soon. I'm going to rock your world when I get you naked."

"Christ, the things that come out of your mouth." She laughed. Just threw back her head and laughed like it caught her off guard. When she looked at him, he had to smile. The mirth on her face was something that he'd never forget. She was so lovely that he couldn't remember a time in his life when she wasn't a part of it. It was like he'd been waiting for her his entire life. "I love you, Sen. So very much that I don't know what to do with all this love that I have for you."

"Thank you." The drive back to her place was a little tricky. The weather had changed again from rain to frozen ice. The roads were slick in places, but it was the black ice that had him taking his time on the way. He was so tense when they got back to the new house that he had to sit in the driveway for several minutes to calm himself down, and he thought for sure that it was going to take him forever to get back under the wheel. "I don't care for this kind of weather. I'm going to have to get myself a better car with Four Wheel Drive soon so that I can get out and about without any trouble. Do you have a car?"

"I do, remember?" He said that he did remember now. "I don't drive much. Usually, I just walk everywhere I want to be. However, with this weather, I have been driving more. And like you, it makes me tense when I have to drive when it's nasty out."

"Then it's settled. We'll get ourselves a new car each with Four Wheel Drive so that we can get around in the weather. Also, in the spring, the weather is nasty too, with all the rain and melting snow. I suppose we'll need to get used to driving in this with the new cars again. I've never had a new car before." She said that her car was the first one she'd ever gotten when she started driving. "You must take good care of it. I never would have thought it was that old."

They made their way into the condo, and he salted the walkway that led up to the place. It was like the road was slick, and he almost fell twice when going up the stairs. He was worried about what the morning would bring, with it getting colder throughout the night. They were calling for snow, and he could believe it, but the report said only a dusting, and as it stood right now, they had that much and more on the walkway. He shoveled off what was there as he salted the walks. He didn't want Sen to fall just because it was cold outside.

After putting away the shovel, glad that there was enough salt around to get all the walks cleaned off, he made sure that things were safe for the two of them when they went into his condo. Locking up the doors, he was happy to remember that he had a security system in the condo and cameras all around the place in the event that Debra came around. And she would, too, of that he had no doubt. And she'd be gunning for Sen when she did, too. That scared him so much that he thought that he'd not get any sleep worrying about it.

Then he remembered that she'd not know where he lived. That took a load of worry off his shoulders, and he was glad that he had talked her into coming to his place. The condo was smaller than her home, but it was cleaned up and there wasn't any kind of mess in the rooms. Plus, the sheets had been put in the washer since she'd wanted clean sheets on all the beds. His place already had that, and he was glad that he'd taken the time to get them in the washer and changed out.

Chapter 6

Sen loved the little place. It was neat, like she liked things, and there was enough room in the place that she could spread out if she wanted. All she wanted now was to go to bed with Ivan and make love all night. However, they were both stressed out from driving, and her mother, so they talked about how things were going with her inheritance. He told her what he thought about her mother, too.

"She's dangerous, isn't she?" Sen told him that she'd not noticed that before, as she'd been the only one dealing with her. "I can see that. You'd have to be on your toes all the time when she was around."

"Not only that, but she's simply too stressful to be around for any reason. Like having a meal with her is a nightmare. She makes demands of not just me when we go out, but of the staff, too. I'm sure that they spit in her food. I would if I had to deal with her. I'm picky too, but she's off the charts in having things done her way." She said she was just a normal picky in that she ate the same things all the time. "Yes, but mother would demand that they take things out of her salad, like cucumbers and onions, and tell them she wanted things like scallops and shrimp in it as a free replacement. Like her substituting things out was the same price as the side salad was in the first place. She would drive me crazy with her demands."

"That's why you ordered for her when we had lunch with her the other day. So that she'd not make a scene. I understand that now." She said if she hadn't been so shocked, she might well have taken exception to her ordering for her. "I can see that too. I think she likes drama so long as it's not pointed at her all the time."

"True. She loves to cause drama between people, but doesn't want bad attention on herself. That makes her angry." She pretended to think about what she said. "No, I think it really pisses her off when things don't go her way. Especially when things don't go her way. That really pisses her off. She huffs a lot, too. That usually gets her what she wants when she makes a fuss about something like that. I've known her to get herself in a better position in grocery lines when she huffs and puffs at people in front of her."

"Christ, she's worse than I thought." Sen told him that she was far worse than anyone ever realized. "I'm glad that you're keeping away from her. I find her threats of killing you scary. I believe that she will try to do it too. She seems like the type that would think she was justified in doing the job, too, because you got more than her. I think you were right in not telling her about the money. She'd kill you simply because she would feel that it belonged to her, because she was your mother. I think that's why she goes on about Robert being her brother. Because that's supposed to be justified in her mind."

"I get that as well." Sen didn't want to talk about her mother anymore and told Ivan that. "I just want to have a nice evening with you and hang out. She's not allowed to be a part of this part of our lives. If we talk about her, that makes what she does seem to be all right. And it's far from all right."

"I agree. Let's go to the bedroom and make love all night." Ivan wiggled his brows at her, and she had to laugh. "There's the laughter that I've been hoping for. You're very beautiful when you smile or laugh. I love the way that your eyes sparkle when you laugh, too."

"I haven't had much of an occasion to think things were funny with all this going on about my family." She looked up at Ivan, who was several inches taller than her. "I love you so much. We're going to be happy for a long time, don't you think?"

"I know that we're going to be happy for the rest of our lives together. Tomorrow we'll find us a forever home and if you wish, raise children together to be happy little people that grow up to be fantastic adults." She said she wanted several children so they'd not be only children. "I understand that. It must have been hard being an only child when you were growing up. I don't know what I'd do without my brothers around. They're my world, and now you are too."

When he pulled her into his arms, she let him. It was nice being close to him, and when he ran his hands up and down her back, she could feel the tension that she had go away. Everything about this man made her feel better, and she couldn't believe how lucky she was in having him in her life. Now, only if she could get rid of her mother, she'd be about as happy as she'd ever been before. And that was spending time without her mother, but with her uncle and aunt.

The bed was made, which she didn't know why, but it surprised her. He was organized as much as she was, so it made sense that his bed was made. She made hers as soon as she got up in the morning as well. She hated to get into a bed that wasn't made up. Sen put her arms up and over his shoulders as he stood there. As he unbuttoned her blouse, she watched his face. Christ, she was so in love with this man that it took her breath away when she thought about it.

When he kissed her, passion was high, and she could feel his erection through his pants, and she moved closer to him. As soon as he cupped her ass, pulling her closer to his body, she moaned out loud and was surprised that his own moan made her wet with need. Everything about this man made her want more of him.

As he pulled at her clothing, she did the same to him. Sen wanted him naked and inside of her now, and she didn't want to waste any time in waiting for him to get around to doing so. Giddy with the knowledge that they were going to have sex, she nearly slapped him with his belt when she pulled it free of his pants. His laughter made her slightly embarrassed.

"How about if we get ourselves undressed that way we won't hurt one another." She said she was in a hurry because she wanted him so badly. "And I want you. However, I don't want to hurt you because my wolf wants you naked as well. He wants to tear at your clothing so that I can have you."

"He sounds like a man or wolf after my own heart." Taking a step back from him, she hurried to undress. Before she could get her pants off, she looked at Ivan and watched as he slowly took off his jeans. Leaving his briefs on, she watched as the dark head of his cock peeked above them. She wanted to taste him in the worst sort of way and licked her suddenly dry lips. Watching him pull his pants off with his socks, it was all she could do to not toss him back on the bed and have his cock in her mouth. Then she thought, why not?

"I want you." Sen pushed him back against the bed and watched as he laid there with his arms above his head. He made no effort to stop her when she crawled to his legs and spread them wide. Getting in the perfect position to have his cock in her mouth, she ran her hands up and down his thighs until she was ready. "I've never done this before. So you'll have to be patient with me."

"You touch me with your mouth, and I'm going to about come all over you. The very thought of you sucking on my cock has my balls up close to my body and aching to empty all over you." She shivered at his words and promises, and she moved closer to where she wanted to be. Pulling his briefs over his erection, she watched as it bobbed slightly and more of his cream leaked from the top. Wanting to taste him, she licked him from root to tip and then took him in her mouth. "Christ, yes, baby. That's it."

She didn't know what she was doing, but he seemed to be enjoying himself, so she continued doing what she wanted. His precum tasted salty and hot, so she lapped up as much as she could. When she put her hands around his cock, he came up off the bed so quickly that he startled her, and all she could do was watch as his cock seemed to pulsate. Pushing him back down, she was happy to see that he was sweating. She'd never realized that foreplay could be so exhausting when you were having so much fun.

Putting her mouth over him again, she traced her tongue around the crown as she fucked him with her mouth. As he began to fuck her too, sliding in and out of her mouth, she nearly gagged when he got too close to her throat. But when she swallowed, and he went past the tightness of her throat, she nearly screamed when he fucked her harder. Christ. Nothing had ever felt this good when she'd had sex before. When he pulled free, she nearly cried out for him to go back when he fisted his own cock and came all over her mouth and face.

Nothing could have prepared her for the climax that she had while he was coming on her. She screamed out loud, rubbing his cream and juices over her body as she came a second, then a third time. Before she could gather her wits about her and tell him how much she loved him, she found herself airborne and landing on the bed, lying on her belly. As soon as the bed moved, she felt the jeans she'd had on being ripped from her body and his hands all over her ass. When he kissed her there, she nearly came again; her body was on fire for him, and she wanted him now.

With his cock at her entrance, she held her breath for what he'd do to her now. As soon as she slammed forward, causing her to be dizzy with the need that suddenly punched her in the gut, she held on tightly as he fucked her from behind. When he reached under her and grabbed her breast, she cried out with pain and pleasure and begged him for more. He gave it to her and so much more than she'd ever experienced before.

"I'm going to bite you." Her body gushed with cream, she could feel it dripping down her thighs. "When I do, I'm going to mark you as mine, and you'll love it. Magic will come to you, too."

"I don't care. Just do it." She felt his tongue, rough and long, slide along her shoulder until he got to her neck. When he licked her again, scraping his teeth along the area, she braced herself for what she knew was coming and screamed until she passed out when he sank his teeth into her flesh. She could have only been out for a few seconds because he was still fucking her hard when she woke. The pain was still there, but not nearly as bad as she thought it would be.

Just as she was going to beg him to let her come, he slid his hand down her body to her pussy and pressed hard against her clit. Her entire body came apart, and she snapped out in the darkness, sure never to be the same again.

When she woke up, she was in the middle of the bed and alone. While trying to move, just to sit up, she hurt in more places than she thought possible. Ivan was just coming out of the bathroom when she was finally sitting up. She smiled back at him when he smiled at her.

"Are you all right?" She nodded, then realized how much that hurt, and told him no, she wasn't. "Neither am I. I didn't think I was going to be able to make it to the bathroom just now. I don't know how this usually works, but you must have gotten your magic while you were out. Scared me a bit when you started crying about the pain. I'm glad that I knew you'd get it, or I might have called someone to come and see about you. While I don't know what it is that you can do with it now, I just know that you got it."

When he climbed into bed with her, she nearly begged him not to touch her. Every part of her body was sore, and she was sure that when she got up to use the bathroom, she was going to be sobbing. Even to wiggle her toes hurt her. She wondered if they made love like that all the time, if she'd be able to survive it. She didn't believe so.

Sen finally had to get up and go to the bathroom. On her way there, she told herself that she wasn't going to cry like a little baby. Sitting on the commode, she did let a few tears fall because she couldn't believe how sore she was, but making her way back to the bed, she did feel better like moving around wasn't so bad as it had been before.

Climbing into the bed with Ivan, she noticed

that he was already asleep. Trying not to disturb him too much, she got in and stayed on her side of the big bed. Almost as if he knew that she was cold, he pulled her into his arms and held her. That was all it took for her to know she was safe and sound and loved. Curling her body around his, she laid her head on his chest and could hear his heart beating. It was so calming to hear it that she found herself drifting off. Sen had never in her life felt as secure as she did right now and wondered if he really would lay down his life for her if the time came.

However, she didn't know what she'd do without him, so she hoped that never happened. She was deeply in love with the man who had not only taken her heart but her body as well. Sen would love him forever, and she knew that he'd love her too.

~*~

Ivan watched the dog's breathing and counted the heartbeats. Her name was Sophie, and she was dying. It broke his heart that such a well-loved dog was suffering so much, but the family wanted to wait on the younger boy, the one who loved her the most, to be there when she took her last breath. It was hard on the others to watch her suffer, but he knew too that she'd want to have her best friend there with her when she passed on. As soon as she wagged her tail, though slowly, he knew that she was smelling her human friend.

"Oh, Sophie." The boy hugged her, and when her heart rate went up, he knew that it was a sort of false hope for her to make it. But she was old. Nearly twenty years old and well past her prime. "Hey, girl. How you doing?"

The boy was far from being a child, so he explained to him that her heart was giving out and that she was just exhausted from living for as long as she had. He told him that he didn't think she was suffering very much, but she was in pain. When he'd tried to touch her belly, she cried out like he'd hurt her.

"Can you give her something for the pain? I don't want her to suffer at all. She's always been there for me since I was five years old." He said he could give her something for it, but he wasn't sure that it would bring her to the end faster. "I'm here with her now. Just make it so that she's not in pain. I don't think I could stand myself if I were to allow her to hurt like she is. She's my best friend. And as much as I'd like to keep her around, I knew this day was coming."

Ivan did what they asked, and he could hear her heart slowing down more. She was tired, and it broke his heart that she was going to die today. Almost as soon as he gave her the injection, the young man said he wanted to stay with her until the end. Handing him the stethoscope so that he could hear her heartbeat, the sign of love if he'd ever heard of, he left them in the room.

As if all the other animals in the waiting room knew that Sophie was drawing to the end, they were quiet and subdued. He didn't want to be busy with another patient when Sophie drew in her last breath, so he asked his nurses if they could set up the next patient. Almost as soon as he thought that he could go in and give shots to his next dog, the young man came out of the room and said she was gone. Ivan felt his own eyes fill with tears as he thought about the young man and his lost friend.

They made arrangements to have her body cremated. Since he had a place where he was going to bury the cremains, he made arrangements to have them shipped directly to the home of the young man. He said he was going to bury them under their favorite tree, and that was where he'd go when he wanted to talk to her. Ivan had a feeling that the young man would be going there daily for a while and then less as the pain went away. But he'd never forget the dog nor any of the time that they spent together as best friends.

The rest of the day went as usual. He had three kittens that he needed to give shots to, so that was something. The family was going to give the kittens away, and he was glad that they were getting them the first set of shots. It would make it easier on the family that took them, knowing that. He also set up a file for the three of them so that if they brought the kittens back in for the rest of their shots, he'd have a file all ready to go. Ivan didn't have names yet, but he knew that he'd remember the files when they did come in.

By the time he was ready to close up for the day, he'd seen twenty-two patients. It was a record for him, and he didn't mind. There had been three more litters of cats brought in to be checked out and a litter of puppies that had been born in his office. He loved it when he could deliver babies into the world. He was sure it was much like the doctors who treated people when they had one to deliver. However, his came in groups and that made it all that much more fun for him. Momma and the babies were doing fine, too.

As he started his walk home, he couldn't believe the weather. It had turned warm overnight and had continued during the day. It was a balmy seventy-three degrees today, and he loved it. He was a spring and fall sort of person, but loved the other two seasons as well. Letting himself into his condo, he was surprised to see Sen there as she said that she was going to go shopping for some things that she needed for the other house. The one she'd gotten from her uncle and aunt.

"I can't stand to be there. It's not the house that is making me crazy, but all the memories that I have there. And my goodness, do I have a lot of them." She held onto him while she told him of all the times that she'd been there and how much she'd loved it. "All I can think about when I'm there is how much I miss them both and wish they were still around. I want a different house, one that you and I can make our own memories in. Is that all right with you?"

"Whatever you want is good with me. I do have a couple of more houses that we can look at when we go out tonight. Did you eat a late lunch like we said we'd do? That way we can get dinner afterwards." She said that she'd eaten lunch at three this afternoon. "That's when I had lunch too, so we should be fine. I'll change, and we'll get going."

He loved how much they seemed to fit with one another. She'd made up the bed in his room and had also cleaned up the kitchen. He would have done it, but they'd both overslept this morning, and he'd been a little too sore to move around that much. As the day went on, he got around better, but he'd bet anything that if they made love like that again, he wasn't going to move for a month. He'd been that sore all over his body, including his hair. He was about to ask her when she turned to him with a huge smile on her face.

"What's going on?" She said that she'd only just realized that she loved him again. "I'm glad to hear that. I love you as well."

He pulled her into his arms and kissed her. It

was such a simple word, a kiss, but it meant so much more than that. He could kiss her all day and not get enough of her, and he knew that she felt the same way, as she'd told him that just this morning. Having a mate was a good deal better than he thought it would be, and he was so glad that Devlin had talked him into going with him when he'd met her for dinner.

They went to the first house on the list and were disappointed. For the area the house was in, it was small and had too many things wrong with it. Not only did it need to have the kitchen redone, which most houses needed, but it also had worn-out old carpet that had holes worn it in all over the house. They talked about carpet, and neither of them liked it in their home. That was good. Ivan thought that if your feet got cold, you should put on socks. It's what he wore all winter long when he was at home by himself.

The second house wasn't much better. But instead of the house needing repair, it was the yard. There were two large vehicles in the yard that were a part of the house they'd been told. So if they wanted to get rid of them, it would be at their expense. Neither of them went through the house very much. With the vehicles in the yard, it was going to be hard to sell the place, and he didn't want to have to mess with it.

They were on the third house when they decided that they were going to get some dinner real quick. They ended up at the pizza shop and ordered two meatball subs. Sen said that she couldn't eat all that much, but he was willing to eat what she didn't. As soon as they were put in front of them, he knew that he'd be lucky to finish his own for the size of them. They were about fourteen inches long and had as many as a dozen good-sized meatballs on them, and he was happy. One of his favorite types of subs was meatball, and he was glad that it was that they decided on.

After their dinner, they went to the last house on their list. The yard was in wonderful shape, and not a single car on the land. There were bushes coming from the driveway to the house, and they were still decorated with lights from the holiday. The man, Mr. Monroe, said that they left the lights on them year-round because it made it easier to see when they were walking up the sidewalk. He decided that he was going to do the same thing because it made sense. Glad now that they had come to the house, they were shown the inside of the house, and both he and Sen fell in love with it. The house was a perfect mixture of old and new, and he loved the fact that it had five bedrooms as well as four and a half bathrooms. It would be perfect for getting ready in the morning if they ever had kids. Not to mention the kitchen was in good shape as well. They'd just have to find them a cook, as they decided that the house was too large for just the two of them trying to keep up with the cleaning.

"It's perfect." Mrs. Monroe said that they were getting to the point where they needed fewer stairs, and that was the only reason they were selling. "I can see that. There are two flights of them to the upper floors."

"There is a washer-dryer set on both floors, so that makes it easy when doing laundry. I loved the fact that I didn't have to carry the kids' clothing upstairs when I finished it. But they've all grown up now, and we're just too old to be living here alone anymore." She laughed a little. "I don't think we're that old, but we do need less space now that everyone has moved out. I miss them being here, but we do get together for the holidays. This is the most wonderful house during the holidays because there is so much room."

"I can see us living here. If the price isn't so bad. How much are you asking for it?" She told him a price that was much lower than he'd thought. "Since you're selling it on your own, how does this work? I've never had to buy a house before."

"We have attorneys who can look over the contract with you. Unless you have one of your own." It was Sen who told the Monroes that they had a lawyer in the family. "That's wonderful. You can have him look things over and then get back with us. Other than going to the bank to sign things over, that's pretty much it. You'll own the house, and we'll be on our way to living in a condo so we don't have to work so hard. I hope you can get it."

He didn't see any problems with them getting the house. With his income and savings, and with Sen having so much money, they could probably pay cash for the house, and it wouldn't hurt them at all. But he knew better than to do that because it was good to use the bank for such things. As soon as they had the contract in hand, they headed to Devlin's condo to have him look it over. He asked for a couple of days, and they said that would be fine.

They didn't have much to pack up to take with them other than the things that he had in storage that he'd gotten at some auctions. With spring coming up, they'd have to hit some more of them in order to fill out their new home. Ivan didn't doubt at all that they'd be able to get the house, so he was excited to have his brother going over the working contract for them so that they could move in sooner. Then he remembered Sen's home, which was left to her.

"We could fill out most of the house with what was left there for you." She said she'd not thought of that and was glad that he'd mentioned it. "The only thing that we might have to get is some new mattresses and a few more linens to take with us, and we'll be set. It'll be nice to have the house looking like a home so soon after we move in, and I'm excited about that."

"I am as well. As I said, there are only a few things that I wanted to get rid of, and that might not happen now. With so much room, we'll be able to fill out the house with those pieces that no one will see. I'm sure that they'll look good someplace in the house." After leaving his brother's condo, they headed to his. They'd been staying there since her mother was out looking for her, and thought it was safer. "We'll have us a lovely home, one like you said we can make our own memories in. I'm happiest about making all kinds of memories with you by my side as I am about anything that I've ever done before."

They were headed home when Devlin called them. He said that he'd have the contract looked over in the morning, and they were both happy with that. He said that he'd skimmed over it a little and didn't find anything wrong with it so far, so they were happy with that. Time would tell if they were getting a good deal or not.

Chapter 7

Debra wasn't happy. She'd been trying to find out what kind of settlement Sen had gotten from her brother's estate, and no one was cooperating with her. As soon as she thought of something, some way of getting information, they'd take it away from her with a lawsuit by Sen. The girl was going to piss her off more if she kept this up, and she wasn't having it. She was going to pay for the way that she was treating her, or she'd know the reason why.

"There was no way that she didn't get a lot of money. The house alone was worth more than the ten grand that I got." She was beginning to talk to herself more and more of late, and it didn't bother her as much as it used to. "Damned girl is going to pay for the way that she's treating me, or I'm going to have to kill her. I might just do that anyway."

She thought of the man that she said she was going to marry. He wasn't a human, and that alone should have had him killed. But if she had to kill him too, then so be it. She didn't think anyone would care, so long as she had the money that she was sure that Sen had gotten to pay her way out of things. Money would open doors that she'd never had opened for her before. She knew that her daughter wouldn't have any kind of will made out, and as her mother, she would get whatever was left to her. Damn the man who she thought she was going to marry. She'd just have to take him out as well if it came to it.

"I deserve whatever she has, and I'm going to get it too." She thought about her brother and wondered where his head was when he left whatever he'd had to her daughter. "Not that I think there was all that much. They only lived in that tiny house all their lives. Who does that anyway when they could have had bigger?" She thought about the fact that she didn't have a place to stay and blamed that on Sen as well.

The house that she'd lived in for the last twenty-five years had been locked out from her going there. All the locks had been changed, and she didn't have anything to show for her living there. As soon as she got the money, she was going to sue Howard and make sure he paid for what he'd done to her. Not only did she not have a house, but she didn't even have a car to get around in either. That was another thing that Sen was going to be paying for. Her home had been taken from her simply because she couldn't stay out of her business. Howard was going to pay too.

She didn't think it was going to work to call him a pedophile again. Too many years had gone by that anyone would even care. She did think about telling his children and having them go after him, but she didn't know them from anyone and didn't even know their names. For all she knew, they could be dead. It was something that she thought about often, him being off the hook for treating her so badly. And he had too. Giving her the things that he had, then taking them away when Sen stuck her nose into something that didn't concern her. Why did she have to care about her father anyway?

"It wasn't as if he had anything to do with her when she'd been growing up." Not that she had anything to do with her either, but that was beside the point. She'd raised her as best as she could, and she dared anyone to say anything differently. "I hate people. Particularly those who think they know it all."

She thought that she was smart enough to get herself out of any kind of trouble. She'd been doing it most of her life, just jumping from one situation to the next and never having to face any kind of consequences. She liked that too. It kept her out of jail and out of trouble. She knew that she was smart enough to take on her daughter and get what she wanted. It was just a matter of timing. And she was good at that as well.

"Damn it all to fuck and back. Why did she have to talk to her father?" Tonight was going to be the dinner that she was going to talk to him, and she dreaded that. "There are things that he could tell her that won't bode well for me. I hate that man with all the passion of the world."

She didn't much care for her daughter either, but she was going to take care of that, too. Killing her wouldn't be that much of a hardship for her. She never did anything for her in the first place but complain about how she was broke all the time. She was her mother; she should be able to sacrifice some things for her when she wanted them. That's what daughters were supposed to do for their mother.

She didn't actually know what a child did for their mother. Her own mother had never been around when she thought that she needed her. Then, when she had died of cancer when Debra had been sixteen, her father had shipped her off to some other relatives who were to raise her. She never cared for them either. It occurred to her that she didn't like all that many people and knew it was their fault. People just sucked the life out of you if you allowed them to do so, and she knew that for a fact. Just look at what her daughter was doing to her.

As she made her way to the hotel she'd been staying in, she thought about what she needed to do tonight. If she knew where this meeting was going to be happening, she'd crash the party and kill them all. But that had been kept from her as well, and that pissed her off, too. No one was helping her, and Debra didn't like it.

"The least people could do was help me find my daughter so that I can kill her." She'd even gotten herself a gun to use to do the deed. It had taken all her reserve money, but that was going to be well worth it. As soon as she killed them all off, she'd have all the things that she wanted. She didn't even know what that would be yet, but she was sure it was more than the ten grand that she'd gotten from the estate.

"Why do they call it that? Like it's going to be a great deal to inherit. Estate sounds like it should be millions of dollars, and there is no way that it could be worth that much." They never took vacations, and as far as she knew, the only thing they spent their money on was getting Sen in that posh school so she couldn't get to her. Not that it mattered, she didn't want to have anything to do with her in the first place. "She was just a means to get money from a wealthy man, and look how that turned out for me."

Nothing. She'd gotten a house for sure and a car that was around for her to use whenever she wanted to go someplace. Money in the bank, too, so long as she didn't spend it the first few days of the month. She'd never been on a budget in her life and didn't plan on ever being on one. Money was there to spend, and she did all right with that. Debra was in her room at the hotel when she thought of something else.

Her credit card was nearly at its max, and she didn't know what she'd do if they checked on that. The hotel wasn't even the best around, but it had suited her needs when she needed it. She'd tried to make it so that the bill went to Sen, but they wouldn't do that. It was like everyone was against her in this thing, and she was going to have to make people understand that she was in charge, or they'd better be looking into something that would make her happy. And she wasn't happy at all with anyone right now.

Looking out on the street, she was dismayed to find that no one would help her find Sen. She might have been at the house, but since she didn't have a car, she couldn't get there without a lot of walking. Debra knew that she was out of shape, but didn't care. She wanted things, and someone was going to have to get them for her, or they'd pay. Exercising wasn't even a part of her life, and she hated that she couldn't get around without her car.

She thought that she saw her daughter walking with that man again. She went to get her gun, thinking that she'd just take care of things now, but almost as soon as she got back to the window, they were both gone. All she needed was one shot, and she'd be able to get all that she needed. Damn her daughter for going against her in everything that she had wanted.

As she stood in the window looking for where Sen might have gone, she thought of all the ways that she was going to spend the money that she had. She knew that there had to be enough to get her someplace to stay, at least for a while. Debra was just thinking about the amount there might be when her head sort of buzzed a bit.

"It's me, the monster you call me. Ivan Frazier." She didn't say anything but did look around for someone in the room with her. *"I'm not there but safe and sound so that you can't shoot either of us."*

"How are you doing this? I demand to know how you're talking to me when you're not around." She looked under the bed and in the bathroom for the man but couldn't find him. "What are you doing to me?"

"I'm not doing anything to you just yet. But you'll be happy to know that as soon as tomorrow, Sen and I will be married, and the will is already made out. If anything happens to her, I get her money and home. And if something were to happen to me, then all her money would go to charity. You'll get nothing." She said that she'd see about that. *"You go on thinking that and see where you end up after trying to kill us."*

"I won't try, but I will kill you both. And anyone else who gets in my way. I have a gun now, and I'm not afraid to use it on you two." She continued to look around the room, knowing on some level that he had to be in the room with her. He'd said that they had a connection, but she still didn't know what that meant. "I want you to stop this nonsense and give me what I have coming."

"That would be my pleasure." She didn't know why he thought that was funny, but his laughter got on her nerves. *"I do believe that you'll get everything you deserve but might not want. So long as you're out of our lives, I can live with killing you myself. I told you that I was a wolf, and that alone should scare you into leaving us alone. I'm not one to fuck with. Nor is my family."*

"There's a whole family of you monsters? Christ, what is this world coming to when people like you can run around free like you're regular people?" She laughed to herself. "If I were to kill the lot of you, people might give me an award or something. Just to have you monsters out of our lives. I'm supposing that you'll want to have children with my daughter. Not that it's going to happen. You'll be dead before that happens."

"Yes, we plan on having children. That'll make you a grandma, not that they'll ever get to know you. I'm going to rip your throat out as soon as you make a move toward Sen. She's my world, and I plan on protecting her with my life." She told him it would come to that, but he'd be dead as well. *"I don't think so. I've got a connection to you now,*

and I can keep you from getting too close to us. I'm under the opinion that you're just too stupid to know when you've lost and end up getting arrested before too much longer. I'd like to know that you're in jail. No more looking over our shoulders every time you're thinking of shooting us."

"I'm going to enjoy you being dead, too. That way, I can get whatever my brother left to her. He shouldn't have done that. He had to know that I'd not be happy with that." Ivan, or whatever his name was, said that he did more than likely know, and that was why he'd taken precautions. "Like what? Was there more money than the ten grand that I got? I just knew it. The dirty bastard left her more than he gave me. I should have pulled the plug on him sooner had I known that."

"Not that it would have changed things. He still would have left her what he did." She asked him how much he'd left her. *"None of your business. Suffice it to say she's got enough to live on for the rest of her life."*

"I'll find out. Mark my words, I'll find out soon, and then you won't have your little secrets around me." She looked out the window again and saw the two of them. When they both turned and waved at her, she knew that she was going to have to kill them soon. They were going to deserve whatever she gave them, and that was going to be it. "I loathe you and my daughter. It's going to give me such pleasure to kill you both. Something that I should have done the first time I saw you."

Her gun was on the bed then, and she knew that if she went to get it, they'd be gone again. She had a feeling that they could make themselves disappear, like in those books that she'd heard about. Shifters were all kinds of magical, and she wished that he'd just die so that she could get on with her life. Damn, but she hated people nowadays. They did nothing but fuck up her life when she wanted things to go her way.

She watched them disappear inside of a car. He'd even made sure that Sen was in the car first and closed the door. Debra knew that he was just showing off; no one of his kind would treat someone like he was Sen unless he'd been raised by humans. Shifters didn't act like that; they were all monsters.

"I'll get you both. And when I do, I'm going to enjoy myself in rolling in the money that should have been mine." Damn her brother for treating her this way. Had she known what he'd been up to, she might well have killed them both herself. Both of them deserved to die, and she was glad that they were gone. "When I get your money, Sen, I'm going to spend it all at one time. Perhaps I'll buy myself something and burn it just knowing that you can't have it. Bitch."

~*~

Howard was nervous. He'd been around Serenity

before. A lot, as a matter of fact, but this was the first time they were together when she knew what he was to her. As her dad, he didn't know what she might expect of him. Not that it mattered, he was going to give her anything and everything she wanted if he could get it for her.

Standing up when she came into the room, he marveled at how beautiful she was again. But she practically glowed when she looked at the man with her. Ivan Fraizer had taken her heart, and he found that he was slightly jealous of the younger man.

"Mr. Bash. I'm glad to meet you finally." They shook hands, and he was pleased that the man had a good handshake. "We wanted to let you know that we're getting married in the morning at the courthouse, and if you'd like to be there, we'd welcome you with open arms."

"Thank you, Ivan. I think I'll take you up on that. I would love to be there when my daughter gets married." He smiled then. "I'm going to pay for dinner for all of us since I saved so much money on the wedding." They all laughed and agreed with him that he'd saved a bit of money.

"I'm just glad to know that you're around. I had guessed that you were my father, but since I didn't ask anyone, I never knew." Serenity hugged him, and he felt good about that. "I'm going to call you Dad, as

I've never said that to anyone before. I hope you don't mind."

"Not at all. It does my heart good to be called dad by you." He felt his eyes fill with tears and let them fall. He didn't know what he was going to do today, but having her in his life now was going to be something that he would love for the rest of his days. "I'm glad to hear that you've found someone to love you. There is no other feeling like that in the world."

"Did you love your wife?" He said that he had at first, but after ten years or so, they decided that they'd made a mistake in marrying. "Then my mom came along and ruined you for other women. She has that effect on people. Causing them harm enough that they don't trust anyone anymore. I know she did that to me."

"Your mother was a lot of things, but nice wasn't one of them." She had to agree, then told him about their encounter with her on their way here. "She's got a gun now? That's scary. I wouldn't trust her with anything. So you be careful out there. I can't lose you after getting you in my life after all this time."

"I have a feeling that you've been some part of my life for all of mine. Isn't that so?" He was embarrassed a little and told her that he'd been a part of everything that she'd done. "I'm thinking, too, that you had something to do with my job, too. I got picked out to take it over about fifty people who had more experience than I did. How well did you know the judge?"

"Smart girl on top of everything else, aren't you?" He laughed. "The judge and I have been friends since your uncle introduced us. He's also the one who got me out of trouble with your mother, too. I owe him a great deal."

"He's the reason that Ivan and I got to meet. He told his brother that I would need an attorney for the reading of the will, and I got to meet Ivan because of Devlin. I'm forever grateful for him telling me I needed help, too. I wouldn't have been so calm about learning about my sudden wealth without him there." Howard asked if she'd gotten everything. "I did, but for ten grand that went to my mother. As you can well imagine, she's none too happy with me for her getting nothing. She knows nothing about the amount I got, but she wants it all. I'm afraid of her if you want to know the truth."

"As you well should be. She's dangerous. Not only that, but she's selfish as well. And that combination alone is deadly to anyone who crosses her." He decided that they'd spent enough time on Debra and changed the subject. "So, how are you finding being a wealthy young woman? I'm betting that you've not spent a dime of it, have you?"

"We bought a house." That was news to him; he thought that she'd been left a home in the estate and asked her about it. "They did leave me their home, but I don't care for it. It's the kitchen for starters, and the memories about the house are too much. I love that they left it to me, but I want something that I'll be able to make memories of my own in. Something that will be our forever home. If you know anything about the place, you know too what a maze it is."

"They tried to make that work for them, but they just couldn't get it right. I tried to get them to sell it; they could have well afforded a newer home, but they said that they were going to work on it until they died. I guess they did at that. However, they didn't want to leave the house for someone else to be upset about, and that's why they stayed there. Even the additions to the house didn't improve it all that much." She asked him if they'd really disliked the house. "Oh, for sure. And when we talked about it, we said how they hoped you'd sell it and get something more for yourself. I think they'd be pleased with your decisions and getting a new home."

"It's not too far from here. It's within walking distance of the downtown area as well. And it has a bit of land that goes with it." He asked for the address and was told it. Howard did wonder if she would have told Debra if she asked, too, and decided that she wouldn't.

She said that she didn't trust her mother, and with good reason. He didn't think that she'd be that forthcoming of her address if Debra was threatening them with shooting them. "You'll have to come and visit us when we get moved in. The other couple, the Monroes, said that they'd be out in a few weeks. They'd already started packing their things up since they put it on the market."

"I'll be happy to see your new home." He found that he was delighted that she wanted to spend any time with him, and he was going to take it when he could get it. "I will have to move closer to you so that we can have a relationship now. I've been living in a rental since my divorce, and it's time that I got myself something else to live in."

"I have a condo if that's the way you want to go. It's two bedrooms and a nice kitchen. I'd gladly let you have it if you want." He said he'd think about that, knowing that he'd take the condo over having to look for a house anytime. "My brother lives not too far away from the one that I had. But he's looking for a house now as well. I think he figures that he's going to need a house when his mate comes along anyway, he might as well find one to start with."

"That's wonderful news." He told him that the condo wasn't too far from their house, either, so he'd be able to walk there when he wanted to visit. "That's even better news. I love to walk. I keep getting my steps in every day so that I can keep in shape. No point in my getting out of shape this late in my life."

They talked about her childhood, and he told her how he'd paid for her school. She seemed to think it was her uncle, and he was all right with that. She'd been such a good student that when she'd gone to college like she had, there was money for her to use as well. He also showed her the pictures that he had of her from a baby to adulthood.

"Robert was really good at making sure I knew a lot about you. When he'd get your school pictures, he'd share them with me. I have a box full of things that you did while in school that he gave me. He was a good man and one that I'm going to miss a great deal." She told him how she had loved them both and that she, too, was going to miss them. "They were a great couple, the two of them. And they provided me with enough information over the years that I knew more about you than I think your mother ever did."

"Once I was sent away to school, she never had anything to do with me. Never once did she visit me at the school, nor did she come to any of the plays I was in." She smiled, such a sad smile that he wanted to hold her in his arms. "Uncle Robert was there for everything. Aunt Cindy, too, when she didn't have plans. Her work kept her on her toes for a long time, I guess."

"Your aunt was devoted to her job. She was good at it, too." She asked if she'd been able to retire from working as a nurse for the emergency department at the local hospital. "I don't think she planned on ever retiring. She always said that she'd die first. I guess she was right. I miss Cindy so much as well." They didn't say anything for a while, and then they were called to dinner. He had only noticed then that the two of them were the only two in the living room where they'd been talking. He appreciated the time alone with his daughter. "Do you suppose we bored them by talking about our lives apart?"

"I heard from Ivan, and he told me that they were enjoying themselves in the kitchen. He told me that it was the place where they met when they had things to talk about. It's going to be the heart of our home, too, I hope. We're going to have to hire staff to keep up with the house; it's bigger than I thought when we started touring it." He asked her if they were taking the furniture from her other home. "Most of it. I really like the things that they collected over the years, and I want to tell any children that we have about their great aunt and uncle. The memories were hard at the house, but I think I'll be fine with a place of my own. Besides, as I said, the house wasn't meant to be for a family. It was just too hard to get around."

"I agree." They went into the dining room together, and he was surprised to see that the family was all there. They must have come in while he was getting to know his daughter, and he was delighted to be able to meet all of Ivan's family. They were a big group of men, and he liked them immediately. "My goodness, it must have been hard on your family to feed the six of you. You're hard to feed now, I'm betting."

He didn't know what he'd said, but it was Ivan who told him how they'd come from an abusive family. He was also told how their mother had killed their father and an officer when she'd been trying to blame them for his murder. They each had a story to tell about their parents, and he was sorry that he'd said what he had. They assured him that he was all right; how was he supposed to know, but he did feel bad for bringing the room down a little. However, it wasn't long before they were in a great mood again, and he enjoyed himself.

When it was time for him to leave, they'd begged him to stay later, but he had things to do; he made his way back to the hotel that he'd been staying in since hearing that Robert and Cindy had been killed. Getting to the desk before going up to his room, he was handed several messages, and all of them were from Debra. Since they were time-stamped with the time that she'd called, he knew, as the notes gathered, she was getting angrier and angrier as she left each note. The last one only said for him to call her, and she'd talk to him, but he wasn't going to do that. He had his own memories that he wanted to have with his daughter, and Debra wasn't going to mess those up with her demands.

Going to bed that night, he was amazed at how much he'd enjoyed himself this evening. He'd not been able to speak to Serenity before like he had tonight, and he had learned a great deal about her. As he rolled to his side to sleep, he wondered if he'd ever get enough of his daughter before she got bored with him and laughed. His daughter was something else, and he couldn't wait to spend time with her now. He doubted that would ever change.

Chapter 8

The movers had brought everything over in two large semi-trucks. Once the furniture was set in a room, they'd move it around once, but that was all. He'd been moving furniture in their bedroom for the past hour. Without Sen's help, it was going slow. Deciding that it was fine for now, he made his way down to the living room, where Sen was directing furniture. The living room looked great, and he wanted to sit down on the nice, comfy couch right now. Ivan found her in the kitchen getting glasses of tea lined up on a tray.

"Here, let me take that. I'm assuming it's going to the movers." She told him that he was right and followed him into the vast room that they were in. "How did you get finished so quickly? This looks amazing." After the tray was emptied, he set it down on the coffee table that he had loved at the other house. "It looks like we've lived here forever instead of just moving in."

"They were very helpful once I knew where the couches were going to go. After that, I just set things up like they were at the house. I think it looks great, too." He picked up one of the lap blankets that he knew had been on the couch in the other house and folded it up. Putting it on the back of the couch, he sat down while the men enjoyed their drinks. "I'm having trouble deciding where to put the bed in our room. I was thinking against the wall where the window is, but that seemed like a bad idea when the sun came up."

"That's where I would have put it. We're both up early anyway, so what does it matter that the sun might wake us?" He told her she had an excellent idea. "Good. One less thing that we have to worry about. The dining room is finished. It was touch-and-go there for a little while. I didn't think the table was going to fit. But once I got the corner cabinets put in and the table set up, it looked really good. We will have to have dinner in there some night. I love how the sun shines in through the stained glass windows that are in there."

The rest of the house was put together quickly because he did what she'd done and set up the bigger furniture first, then put the smaller things around it. It didn't hurt that the rooms here were larger than the rooms at the other house, and there were more rooms as well. Once the last truck was emptied, the movers tipped their hats at Sen, and they were on their way. He was going to give them a good review about how they'd helped move them in today. His family showed up right after the last truck was pulling away.

"We thought we'd come and help you move stuff around, but it looks like you have that handled. Gracious, this looks great. I'd never know that you've been living here all of ten minutes." The rest of his family teased them as well, and he found that he didn't care. Things were being set up, and that's the way that it should be. Lica continued speaking when they were sitting in the living room. "I've heard from my source at the police station. Your mother has been arrested, Sen. She wasn't paying her bill at the hotel she was staying in, and the credit card that she'd given them had been canceled by the company that it was issued from. I'm sorry."

"I'm not." Sen leaned back on the couch they were sitting on and smiled. "You've just given me the best news. I was sick of looking over my shoulder all the time, waiting for her to pop out at any moment."

"She had a gun on her, too. It wasn't registered to her, and it's been taken away. She seemed more upset about that than she did the fact that she was in jail." Sen asked Lica if they knew where she'd gotten the gun. "No. And she's not talking either. I'm assuming that she bought it from the back of some car or something. But when they asked her what she was going to do with it, she said that she had some people that needed to learn their place. She never mentioned you, but I know for a fact that she's been saying that she was going to kill you for the money anyway."

"I didn't want to believe that she'd kill me, but I guess she really would have. When she leaves the jail, will they give it back to her?" It was Devlin who explained that she'd not get it back because it wasn't registered to her. "Good. I'd hate to think that they'd give her a gun as unstable as she is. Maybe she'll cool off now that she's in jail."

"Do you really believe that?" She shook her head and took his hand into hers. "I think that she's going to cause trouble no matter where she is. The boys at the stationhouse are complaining about her wanting to speak to you. I told them that there is no way that you were going to go down there and have anything to do with her. I hope that was right on your part." She nodded at Lica.

"It scares me to no end that she was able to get a gun in the first place. I mean, she's my mother, why on earth does she think that killing me is going to get her anything?" Edmond told her that he'd heard that she was still going on about her brother leaving you everything. While she doesn't know, he told her what the amount is, Debra has a feeling that Sen got a great deal more than she did. "That's true. I did. A great deal more than she did. However, I was told not to tell her that. She'd drain me dry if I were to tell her the things that were left to me and not her. I have a feeling that Uncle Robert knew what she'd do if she found out. I worry now about my father, too. He has money too and has taken her house and car from her."

"I heard about that. I also heard that it's the reason why she beat you so badly when you were a child. She kept you from asking about him again by doing that." Sen said that was why she'd never even asked if the Howard at her uncle's house was her dad or not. Because she knew that she'd get hurt again if she asked, so she never did again. "I thought as much. So this thing with your parents should have ended long ago instead of just now. You were probably lucky in that you didn't ask again. She seems like she would have killed you even back then."

"I never thought about that, her being unstable. I guess I thought that every parent was like her. I had no one to compare her to growing up. All the kids that I went to school with were from divorced parents and had lots of money. I just assumed that everyone had been treated the same way that I had been." Guy said that was very sad to be treated that way. But it might not have been so bad had she been able to live with her father. "I've thought about that. My mom was never really a part of my life until I got out on my own. And even then, it was just for things that I could give to her. She was never good with money and never worked. I had no idea she was getting the money from my father until years later. Even then, she tried to lie to me and said that it wasn't that much. She was making one hundred twenty grand a year, and she was broke by the end of the month. That's truly sad to me. Then she'd come around and want me to take her out to dinner or pay for her nails to be done. Things like that."

"I wonder what she's going to do now that all her extras are gone." Sen told Ayden that she was trying to move in with her. "I'm sure that wouldn't work. The two of you don't get along on the streets. I can't imagine it would be any better in a house with the two of you. Someone would be dead for sure."

"You got that right. She doesn't know that we bought a house yet. I don't plan on telling her, however, she might well see the moving vans outside the house. But she might not have because it was while she was in jail." Sen said that it would be great if that had happened that way. But she didn't believe she had that much luck. "I know that feeling. It seems like when something goes right, ten things go wrong. Like at the office yesterday. I thought I was going to have a good day when all of a sudden everything went wrong. It's why I was so late getting out of the office. Because I had to clean up one mess after another. A dog and a cat threw up in the office, which had to be cleaned up. Then I broke a tube that I was using, full of urine all over my lab coat. It was a day from hell."

"I'm sorry that it happened that way. But we have the house finished up, so we have that going for us. We only need to go to the storage unit and get what you have there, and everything will be done. Yay for us." Ivan kissed her on the nose and told her that with his brothers there, he'd go get it now. They fussed a bit, but he knew in the end that they'd go and do what he wanted. He'd helped them out enough when they had moved in. The only person who wasn't there was Guy because he had a deadline coming up and had to get his book finished.

They were all excited about the next book coming out. It was a murder mystery that was like his Sloan series. Guy had a ghost around that would talk to him, and she had been murdered. It didn't take him long to figure out how she was killed and even less time to figure out who had killed her. So he wrote a book about it, leaving out the part where he saw the ghost of the dead woman that was hanging around him. She moved on when he did, as she had asked him to do, and that was to get Amber, her stepdaughter and mate to him, the insurance money that she'd left for her.

After he and his brothers left to go to the storage unit, they were able to load the three bedroom suites up in their trucks and bring them to his house. They even stuck around to put them together with the mattresses that he'd ordered to go with them. Looking around the bedrooms, he was pleased with the way that they'd turned out and was happier still for the help that he'd gotten from his family. He didn't know what he would have done without them around all the time.

It was Brandy who suggested they order out. She didn't just order for them from one place, that would be too much for one place to handle, but she did order a variety of foods that came from several places. Chinese, pizza, subs, as well as pasta and salads from another place. There was plenty to eat as well as enough of a variety to make sure there was something for everyone. Even Ayden was able to find something in the plethora of food to fill himself up.

It was going on midnight when his family left. They didn't have to get up in the morning, so staying out late was all right with them. He, however, needed to be at the clinic at nine the next morning, so when he went up to bed with Sen, he made sure to set his alarm twice before he fell asleep. With Sen curled up around him, it was wonderful to sleep in their new home together.

He woke up around two to go to the bathroom. On his way back, he stubbed his toe on the bottom of the bed. Moving the furniture around so that that wouldn't happen was going to be something he did in the morning before leaving for work. He knew that might happen and wasn't surprised that it had. Limping to the bed, he was curled up around Sen before he fell asleep again.

Ivan got up before Sen and was out of the shower before she got up. She didn't seem to be in such a good mood all of a sudden, and he asked her about it. She said that she'd not slept all that well last night because she had a lot on her mind. Mostly to do with her mother, but also her dad. She was being pulled in two different directions right now, and he felt sorry for her. He knew that she'd get it all worked out, but for now it was weighing on her heavily.

There was little he could do for her in this; she was the one dealing with her father. He liked the older man a great deal, but there was pressure from him about getting to know Sen. She wanted to get to know him, but she was also worried that her mother was going to get out and hurt her. It was something that he could help her with by talking to the police officers about what she'd said. It would be up to them if she were to get out sooner rather than later, and that worried him as well.

~*~

Sen had a pile of work that she had to catch up on. Glad to be at work, she sailed through most of the files before lunch. Putting the others off until after lunch, she was able to enjoy a nice, quiet lunch by herself in the cafeteria. Since she'd brought leftovers from home, she didn't have to mess with it too much before she got to eat. It was a good day so far, and she was having fun being back at work. Judge Rainer sat down next to her just as she was getting up to go back to work.

"I have a case in the morning that is going to take me away from the office for most of the day. It's hearing the charges against your mother." She asked him if he should be talking to her about it. "I'm just telling you that I'm going to be gone all day tomorrow. Anyway, that has nothing to do with you knowing." He grinned at her.

"She had a gun, did they tell you that? She was planning on killing me with it." He said that's what he'd heard from the jailers. "I'm worried that she's going to be getting out soon and find herself another weapon to do me harm. I just got my life the way that I want it, so I'd really hate to find myself dead because of money."

"I would as well. She's going to have to serve some time with the gun. She's been in prison before, and she's not allowed to have a weapon." She asked when she'd been in prison and what for. "She robbed a convenience store when she was eighteen years old. She didn't spend all that much time in the system, but it was enough to be put on her record. That's going to get her into trouble the most. I'm sorry I can't do anything about her threatening to kill you. Unless, of course, she mentions it in court. Then I can get her for that too. Do you believe that she'll be brazen enough to tell me what she's planning on doing when she gets out?"

"She thinks that she's justified in killing me for the money because he was her brother and only an uncle to me. To be honest, if it wasn't for the fact that she wasn't around them when the accident happened, I'd swear that she killed them both. It would be just like her to get money. She gives me the impression that the money should have come to her in the first place." He said that's what the officers told him when he asked. Like she's privileged or something. "Yes, that's her in a nutshell. She's privileged thinking, and that's what gets her into trouble. My father was giving her ten grand a month to help her keep herself, and she would spend it on things that I have no idea where they might be."

"I'm good at leading someone down the path of being against the law. I'll get her to tell me what she's planning on doing with the gun. I won't give it back to her; she's not allowed to have it, but I will make sure that she can't use it against you when she's out and about. Not that I think she'll be out for a very long time. But I'm pretty good at my job." She told him that she knew that, that's why she loved working with him. "Thank you. I had hoped that you'd say something like that. I thought that now that you're married, you'd quit and stay at home making babies."

"I plan on having children with Ivan. I don't know how many, but a few. But as for working, I don't plan on being a stay-at-home mom for very long. I think I'd go crazy." He told her that was what his wife had said about doing the same thing. "I have enough money now that I could do whatever I want, including becoming an attorney. But I have no desire to do anything like that right now. I'm happy with the way things are going for me and Ivan. As I said, maybe down the road I'll want to try something else, but for now I'm happy."

"Good for you." They walked to the elevator together to go back to work. "The hearing will start at nine in the morning. Can I assume you'll be there?"

"Yes. I wouldn't miss it for the world." They talked about their new home, and she told him how it was finished being unpacked. "Having movers do most of the hard work paid off. I don't think I could have done it any other way and been as happy with the results. Now all I have to do is decide what I want to do with my uncle's home, and I'll be able to move on from there. It's going to be nice having everything done right now. I'm excited to get things moving in the right direction for a change."

"Yes, having money does help in a great many things." She agreed with him. "You do good work, honey, and you'll go far. I'm happy that you're going to be working for me for now, and that's all that I can ask for. We'll talk more after tomorrow. You be safe now."

"I will, and you do the same." He said that he was wearing a bulletproof vest to work nowadays. "I guess that makes sense. I know the world is changing every day in how people react to things. You wear your vest, and I'll be happier for it."

As she started back to work, she found herself wondering if she should invest in a vest as well. Thinking herself silly, she decided that she was going to wear something nice tomorrow instead of the jeans that she had been planning on wearing. She wanted her mother to notice her, notice that she had come up in the world. Sen looked down at the ring that Ivan had given her just this morning at the courthouse when they were married.

They'd been married quickly and quietly. All the families were there, and she loved that most of all. Brandy had been the one to stand up with her, and Ivan had asked Devlin to stand up with him. It was quite an affair, and she was glad that it was finished. Sen was glad that they'd done it this way and that things had gone perfectly for them.

As she finished up her workday, she headed home free of trying to figure out if her mother was going to be there to attack her. Sen had no doubt that her mother would do something that would cause her harm; she just hoped that it was harm rather than killing her. She'd not been kidding when she told Judge Rainer that she didn't want to be looking over her shoulder every minute of every day while she was free to run around.

Going to bed that night, she was happy with the choices that she'd made as to what she was wearing tomorrow. The dress was one that she'd never worn before and had been a part of her aunt's clothing. The price tag had still been on the garment, and she'd paid quite a bit for it. Ivan was going to wear a tie that almost matched the dress perfectly, and she was glad for that. She thought they looked like a power couple, just as she hoped her mother would see them.

The next morning, she was up and ready to go by seven. Her sleep had been pitiful, but she'd gotten enough that she wouldn't be yawning all day. When Ivan came downstairs, she'd already had a bit of breakfast as well as two cups of tea. She was beginning to see the appeal of a good, strong cup of tea and was glad that Ivan liked it as well.

Getting to the courthouse on time, she sat in the

chairs directly behind Devlin at the prosecution table. While this wasn't a trial as yet, he was there to provide as much evidence as would be needed to send her mother away to prison. If nothing else, perhaps she'd be in the jail system for some time before her trial.

When the courtroom was called to order, she stood up with the rest of the people in the room. They'd not brought out her mother as yet, and she was curious what she might look like after spending ten days in jail. Surely they wouldn't allow her to have a hairdresser come in and take care of her needs. With a little laugh, she thought that her mother would have been demanding all kinds of stupid things while she was in the system.

After being seated, the judge made an announcement about how this was a courtroom and that things would be orderly. He also said that this wasn't a trial, just as she'd thought too, and that today would bring order to the lives of so many people. Then her mother was brought out.

She'd not only not had a hairdresser come to her in her hour of need, but it looked like she'd not had her hair washed at all since she'd been put away. Even from as far away as she was, Sen could see that her nails were broken and the polish chipped. In a word, her mother looked horrid. Like being in jail had been the final straw in her not taking care of herself. She couldn't believe how terrible she looked.

After Devlin said what he was there for, the reasons why her mother had been arrested, he handed the judge several files and some to the defendant's table as well. He was saying how she'd been arrested for running up a tab that the hotel was demanding payment for, as well as she'd been found with a gun on her person. Then he went on to say that, as an ex-con, her mother was in violation of her release from prison.

Sen found herself tuning out the proceedings and thinking about her life so far. She had a wonderful husband, a good amount of money, and a home that she loved. If there were more to life than that, she didn't know what it would be. Of course, she did add that having family around was important too, as she thought about how much she loved all of Ivan's family of brothers and their wives. Then she thought about Ivan.

He was a good man and a better friend than she'd ever had. It didn't take her long to figure out how much she loved him, and she was glad for that. Having someone to love was important to everyone, and she thought that she was especially lucky in that Ivan was so good to her. And he was too.

Never once had they had a fight about anything. But then they were new to each other. She found that she would agree with what he would say just to see his smile. And he was happy with his entire face when he did that. His laughter was something that she would look forward to daily. She'd think of silly things all day just to hear him laugh with her about it. Then there was their lovemaking.

It was gentle most of the time, but there were times when she was painfully aware that he'd been a little rough. Not that she minded about that. She would enjoy it as much as he did, like the other morning when he woke her up while eating her.

She'd come up off the bed with a scream to release. He'd been licking her pussy and suckling at her clit for some time if she was honest with herself. He told her to lie back down so that he could finish, and she wanted him to fuck her. But he wasn't taking no for an answer and swatted her on the ass as he fucked her with his tongue.

Coming as hard as she did, Sen was sure that she'd be hoarse come the end of the day. But it was well worth a little sore throat for all the things that he'd given her. And when he finally fucked her, she came again and again until she simply passed out with pleasure. It was something that she would think about forever. The low growl from Ivan had her looking at him.

"I can smell you. Behave, or I'll beat your bottom when we get home." She told him how sorry she was.

"Don't be sorry, just stop doing what you're doing. I won't be able to sit here quietly if you keep that up."

She giggled, bringing attention to her from her mother. When she stood up, so did Sen. They stared at one another for a long, tense-filled moment before her mother was made to sit down again.

"She's the reason that I'm in here." Judge Rainer asked her how she had not been the one to pay the hotel bill. "She got my brother's money, and I didn't. If she had given it to me like I asked, then I'd of not have had to buy the gun to get the money."

"What do you mean, she's the reason that you had to buy the gun? Like the hotel bill, I'm not sure how that even equates to her causing you trouble. Perhaps you'd like to explain yourself." With a glance in her direction, she kept standing when her mother stood again. "Ms. Ranger, I'm waiting for an answer. Why did your daughter have you buy a gun that you knew you weren't able to have?"

"She is going to give me that money, or I'm going to kill her. She thinks she's so smart to keep me out of her bank account, but I have ways of finding out what's going on. My brother should have left his money to me, not to her. She no more deserves it than she does to be alive right now. And she made it so I lost my house and car too, by trying to find her daddy." Again, Judge Rainer asked what she was talking about.

"My daughter got all the money from my brother's estate, and that wasn't right. I was his sister, and that's the way it should have been. When she decided to keep me out of her accounts, I decided that he gave her much more than he did me, and now I'm going to get it from her. Even if I have to kill her. I will too. No matter what you do to me, she's going to die, and so is that husband of hers if they're really married."

"They're married. I did the deed myself. But let's get back to you killing your only child. You said you'd do it. I have it on good authority that you no longer have the gun that you got illegally. Just how are you planning to make that work?" She said it had been easy to get a gun in the first place, and she'd have no trouble again. "So you'll get yourself another gun and try to kill your child and her husband for money. Is that what you're telling me?"

"Yes. And I won't try. I'll kill her dead the first chance I get. She no more deserves his money than I do living the way I'm going to be without funds. She did this to me, and now she's going to have to pay."

Chapter 9

Debra got five years in prison for the gun specification, and her trial for the hotel was going to be in eighteen months. If she lived that long. None of them could see her living that long in prison with her attitude and the way that she spoke to people. She'd be lucky if she made it a year there, and that's fine with him. Ivan liked her being in prison and not out and about.

After making it home from the trial, he encouraged Sen to go up and take a nap. She looked worn out, and he felt bad that she had not slept well the night before. As he laid down with her, telling her that he'd stay until she went to sleep, she told him about the night that her mother had beaten her.

"I'd asked about my father. All the other kids had dads who were either living at home with them or they went to visit him on weekends. Most of my friends were from divorced parents, and that was all right, I guess. But at least they had dads that they could see. I had no one." He asked her if she'd ever talked to Howard at her uncle's house. "Just polite conversations. I'd not figured out who he was just yet, so he was just a friend of my uncle and aunts."

"I heard that you were in the hospital for two weeks. It must have been bad. I'm sorry that you had to go through that." She said that she was as well, but now that she'd had time to think about it, she knew that her mother was trying to kill her. "What would that have gotten her? I wonder if she thought that far ahead. Killing you would have ended all the things that she'd gotten from Howard, don't you think?"

"I think she was so enraged that she didn't think beyond having me not ask about him. I was just a kid wondering why I didn't have what the other kids had, and at first she slapped me." She rolled to her back but didn't look at him as she continued. "Once I was down on the floor, she stomped me so hard that I had four broken ribs. My wrist had been broken as well as my leg when she took something hard and beat me with it. I never knew what it was, but I hurt. Even after I passed out, she continued to beat me until I was nothing left but a bloodied child that didn't understand."

"After that, you were sent to a boarding school, correct?" She told him how she'd not even been healed all the way before being shipped off. "Then your uncle stepped in and took over your care. You'd think that Howard would have had something to say about the way that she'd beaten you."

"I'm not sure he knew all the particulars about what went on that day. And Howard is the one who paid for me to go to boarding school. He told me that just the other day. Uncle Robert is the one who suggested it, but my dad is the one who paid for it. My college too. I'd thought that I'd gotten enough scholarship money to pay for it all, but it was him." Ivan watched as tears streaked down her cheeks. She still wasn't looking at him, and he was all right with that. "When I got out of college and got a place of my own, Mother started coming around me like nothing had happened. I think that's why I didn't remember it all that well. She acted like nothing had hurt me, and I was willing to let her think that. I was afraid of her, even after all that time had passed. I didn't ask about my father again either. Not until my uncle and aunt died."

"I'm sorry that you had to go through all that. The way she was talking in court today, you'd think that she thought it was justified in killing you for the money. I think that scared Judge Rainer, too. He seemed shocked by her just telling him what she planned to do to you. I think that's why he gave her the maximum on the gun thing." She said that he'd talked to her yesterday and told her that he was going to get out of her what she planned to do with the gun. "I believe he got more than he had hoped for, don't you?"

"He's a good man, my boss. He wondered if I was going to quit working for him now that we're married. I assured him that I was going to work for him until I couldn't do it anymore." She finally looked at him. "I don't want to be a stay-at-home mom either. I will work a job with adults and then go home to be with my babies. I know that sounds selfish, but that's what I want to do. I don't think I'd be a good mom if I had to be around the house all day."

"I'll be working too for the same reasons. Lica was going to be a stay-at-home dad with his little one, but after about three weeks of it, he decided that he couldn't do it. He told me that he spent so much time playing with and watching his child that he didn't get anything else done. He needed a break for taking a break from working. I agree with him on that. It would be tough to be around kids all day without adult contact." She told him that was it exactly. "Good. When we have children, we'll hire a nanny to take over during the day while we're at work. Nothing is set in stone with that, so if we, either of us, decide we want to be there with the kids, we can do that as well."

Almost as soon as they decided on that bit of information, she fell to sleep. Ivan watched her for several minutes while she laid there quietly before he got up to see about the household. He needed to get some of the things done that he'd been putting off in favor of spending time with Sen, and he was glad for the time. He went outside before he got caught up in wanting to lie down beside her while she slept.

The day was beautiful. It was almost eighty degrees outside, and there wasn't a cloud in the sky. Spring was in a couple of days, and he couldn't believe the weather they were having. The yard had been taken care of just yesterday by the lawn service, so he had nothing to do when it came to the trimming. However, he did go out to the gardens to see how they were thriving. He was going to the front of the house to do the same when someone pulled into the driveway.

He didn't know the car, but he did know that it wasn't one of his brothers either. As he leaned on the shovel that he'd found in the garden, he watched the doors open. He was surprised that Howard got out of the car and came toward him. There was something about his gait today that had him concerned. He looked pissed off. His smile didn't reach his eyes.

"I was hoping to talk to Serenity. Where is she?" He told him she was taking a nap and that she'd not been sleeping well. "Can you wake her? I really want to talk to her about something. You can listen in, too, but it's going to be between the two of us."

"As I said, she's not been sleeping well, so she needs to have this lie down. Whatever you wish to say to her will have to wait." There was a flash of anger, but he continued to smile at him. Ivan leaned the shovel against the house in the event he had to shift quickly.

He might have to if the man didn't explain why he was so angry. "I can have her call you when she wakes up. I don't know how long she'll be, but I know that she was exhausted when she went to sleep about an hour ago."

"I've come all this way to talk to her, and I'm going to do it even if I have to go into that house and wake her myself." He just stared at him. "You heard me. Get her out here so that I can talk to her about business. Now that her mom is out of the picture, she's going to need someone to keep her in line with the money that I'm going to leave her. She's going to be a very wealthy woman."

"She is now. We both are." Ivan shifted on his feet and was trying to get his own anger under control. He'd never acted like this before and was sort of shocked that he was acting like this now. Something must have happened, and he was going to get to the bottom of it before he allowed him to talk to Sen and piss her off, too. "As I said, she's not been sleeping well, and you're going to have to wait for her to wake up. I'm not going to allow you to go into our home and disturb her."

"We'll just see about that, now won't we?" He started toward the door, and Ivan had had enough. Shifting into his great beast, he stood in front of the door with his fur standing up on end and his teeth bared. He wouldn't get past him without a fight, and

Howard wouldn't live long enough to talk about it when he attacked him. "What do you think you're doing? I'm not going to allow you to treat me this way. I said that I was going to talk to my daughter, and I'm going to do that now. Get out of the way before I have to hurt you."

He stood his ground. Seconds before he was ready to attack, he heard the door behind him open, and there was Sen. He could smell her and her anger, too. Before he could guess what she was going to do, she put her hand in his fur and rubbed his head. It was all he needed to be calmed.

"What's the meaning of this, father?" Howard said that he wanted to talk to her. "I was taking a much-needed nap when I heard raised voices. My hearing is a great deal better than it used to be, so I heard every word. I need to rest, and you're out here threatening my husband. What's the meaning of this anger that you have right now?"

"Your husband wouldn't allow me to talk to you. He, well, he never mentioned that you were taking a nap." She called him a liar, and he looked angry again. "Now see here. I'm your father, and you'll not take that tone with me. I have a business that you're going to be running when I'm no longer able to run it, and it's time to get you acquainted with the people who work for me. Now that your mother is out of the picture, you can come and go as I please and get this taken care of."

"No." He asked her what she meant, and she told him that she was happy with the businesses that she had to run for her uncle. "He left me with enough money that I don't have to work, but I plan on working until I don't want to anymore. It sounds like whatever you have planned for me is going to take me from my job and my new home. I don't need the extra pressure that you're going to be putting on me."

"It's a very profitable business, and I demand that you come with me to learn it. I'm not kidding you right now, Serenity. You'll come with me now and learn everything that you need to so that you can be wealthy beyond your wildest dreams." She told him she already was wealthy beyond anything that she ever dreamed of. "Well, you can't ever have enough money. That's what I told your uncle when he was telling me that he was going to retire. Retirement is for the old and poor. You'll come and learn my business so that when I'm ready to turn it over to you, we can both still make a great deal of money."

"No, I won't. I'm going to go back up to my bedroom and take a long nap. You'll just have to deal with me not doing what you want on your own. And you ever talk to Ivan that way again, I'll have nothing to do with you. Do I make myself clear?" Howard said she was being unreasonable. "Perhaps. But you're the one making demands right now on my time when I'm so exhausted that I want to lie down right here and sleep. Go away and don't come back until you can remember your manners." He didn't take his eyes off of Howard when he heard the door behind him shut.

"Well, that fucking bitch." Howard's face was red; he was so angry, and when he took a step toward the house, he growled low in his throat. Howard didn't move. "You're going to stop me, aren't you? If you do, there is hell going to be paid. Hell, she'd not have this money to buy this house without me around her uncle. Who does she think she is, treating me this way? I've been waiting for a long time for her to be free of her mother, and now she does this to me. I just don't believe it."

There was nothing he could say to the man, but he did watch him. They'd formed no connection the two of them so he couldn't speak to him. The only thing he could do was to keep an eye on him so that he would not try to get into the house. Ivan would kill him if he tried. And right now, it was iffy if he didn't kill him anyway. He didn't know what was going on with the older man, but he didn't trust him at all. Not anymore. There was something wrong with him. Or perhaps it had been there all along, and he'd kept himself in control. Whatever the issue, he wasn't going to get past him and to his mate.

~*~

Howard was sick to his belly when he made his way to his hotel. He'd been holding his temper for so long that he felt like it was a part of him. Now that Debra was out of the way, Serenity should have wanted to spend her time with him. It was the very least she could do since he was her father, damn it. And that man getting in the way, Ivan made him pissed off because he was cockblocking him from his daughter. Well, that wouldn't last, damn it. He'd take care of him right away.

He'd been nice, hadn't he? He'd waited for his turn to spend with his daughter. He'd not even had a fit when she said that she was getting married. A husband working would give her more free time to hang out with him. Howard had thought that Ivan would be manipulative enough for him to get him to do what he wanted. This wasn't turning out the way that he wanted it to, and he was going to have to show them both that he was the one with the money and that what he said was the way things were going to go. No more of this napping because she felt tired. He was tired all the time trying to be the man that she wanted around, and look where it had gotten him. Nowhere. Just on the outside of her life now that her mother was gone.

He should have killed her when he had the

chance. Debra had sucked him dry to the point where he'd had to go back to working full-time just so that he could have disposable income when he needed it. Not that he didn't have enough money to do what he wanted, but it was the principle of the thing. She'd been demanding, and he'd fallen for her lies.

She'd lied to him about a lot of things about his daughter. First and foremost was the fact that he'd be able to see her when he wanted. Then she'd changed her mind and had said that she didn't want her in his life. That little tidbit had been put in the contract without his knowledge. He should have known better than to give her the say-so over the contract that he'd had with her. It wasn't until Debra had nearly killed his daughter that he'd figured out that he was to have nothing to do with her so long as she never asked about him. Damn it, he'd had to fire a good attorney who had worked for him for years when that had been told to him. He should have killed him as well.

Howard thought about all the people that he'd had to kill over his lifetime. It had gotten him to be a wealthy man, of course, but it had come at the cost of blood on his hands. To think that he'd been acting like a good man all these years, and it had gotten him nothing. Not even a good daughter that would see to his needs. What burr was up her ass about doing what he'd wanted her to do? He asked himself that question daily since he'd been able to be a part of her life. Damn it, but he hated his kids. Even his firstborn would have nothing to do with him once he cut them off from his life.

It had been easier than he thought it should have been to tell them that he wanted nothing to do with them. After divorcing their mother, they didn't have much to do with him in the first place. Then, when he'd told them that he was cutting them out of the will as well, they just smiled and walked away. Like they knew something that he didn't. But in all these years, none of them, not a single one of them, had contacted him for money. He knew, too, that they were struggling, and it did his heart good to know that. But they didn't come running to him for a single penny, and that had pissed him off as well.

Howard had wished that he'd never been married. But his father had told him if he didn't marry and have children for him to bounce on his knee before he died, then he'd get nothing of the estate. Marrying the first woman who said yes, he regretted it since the day she said yes. If not for the fact that he needed someone to run his empire, he'd not have a thing to do with Serenity. Women were the ruination of the world as far as he was concerned, and he didn't care who knew it.

He'd been pampering his daughter long enough.

It had made him ill to act like a loving father to her when all he wanted was for her to take over running his companies. But today proved that she was more like all the women he knew than anything.

"A nap. It's the middle of the day. Who takes naps anyway?" He couldn't believe that that man had kept him from going into the house that he'd paid for. "Not really, but if I'd had my way, Robert wouldn't have had a thing to do with my daughter. But at the time, it was all I could do to see her thanks to her mother."

Lying down in the bed so that his head would stop pounding, he decided that he needed something for it. Calling down at the desk, he asked for a doctor to come and see him, and they told him that there was only one doctor who did house calls. For enough money, they'd all god damned make house calls if he wanted. But he played nice again, and after hanging up the phone, he went to the bathroom to throw up. It was mostly bile and blood, but he was used to that. He'd have to play nice for a while, or he'd be back in the hospital, where they'd tell him that he had to control his blood pressure or he'd die.

"Like they know when a person is going to die from a headache." His belly was upset, too, and a doctor at one time told him that he had an ulcer. They'd wanted to take it out, or at least do surgery on it, but he'd have to be laid up for a while, and that wasn't good for him. "It would be like taking a nap during the day. Damn it."

Lying back down, waiting for the doctor, he told himself that he could get over this. However, the longer he laid there, the sicker he got. It wasn't until he was at the toilet again that he realized that his belly was really upset and that there was more blood than bile in his vomit. This couldn't be good, he told himself.

The doctor showed up just as he was contemplating calling an ambulance. Being nice to the man — it was a small town, and things got around quickly about him being a bastard — but he was ill, and he wanted some relief.

"You need to be put on some medication, or this is going to kill you. You said that you've had an ulcer all your life?" He told him that it was just a way for the doctors to make some money off of them. "Well, I'd say it would have been money well spent. I'm going to call an ambulance for you so that we can get some fluids into you. You're not well, and your belly is only going to get worse from here on out."

He didn't have it in him to argue with the man. He really wasn't feeling well and was worried that he'd been too nice for too long. That's what made him ill. Trying to appease his daughter so that she'd do what he wanted. Well, no more. He was going to be Howard the way that he wanted, and damn her sensibilities. Women were too delicate most of the time, and he hated that he'd have to be nice to them to get what he wanted.

By the time the ambulance had arrived, he was sick again. The doctor had insisted on seeing what he threw up from his belly, and that worried him all the more. It was just blood. His body was making more of it even as he threw it up. Everyone knew that. But the worried look on his face had him cooperating with the people from the hospital's ambulance service more than he thought he should have. He was off to the hospital as quickly as he'd ever been.

He thought about calling his daughter as he was being set up in a room. They were putting sticky tabs on his chest and running a test that way. He didn't know what it was called, nor did he care, but so long as they kept giving him something for the pain, he'd do just about anything that they wanted.

He was being run through a donut-shaped machine when the pain started to come back. True to their words, they had told him that he'd not suffer needlessly; he was given something more for the pain. As he was being drugged up, he thought that he could get some sympathy from his daughter and her dumbass husband when they told him that he was going to need surgery. After that, it was a blur of activity to get him prepped so that they could cut him open to see what sort of damage he'd done to himself by being nice.

While he didn't know what they were going to do to him, he agreed that they'd cut him open. When he was taken to surgery, they told him that they'd give him something to knock him out, and that was all he remembered.

Waking up once, he was told that things went well and that he should be in the mend. He didn't have it in him to ask what they were talking about, but he closed his eyes again. Things were too much for him to stay awake, so he let the drugs take him under until he could think. Howard didn't know what they were giving him, but he'd have to find out and invest in it. It was the best thing that he'd ever had when he'd been ill with his belly.

He woke up again, and the room was dark. He didn't know if the shades were drawn or if it was actually dark outside, but he felt like it should be nighttime. Howard knew that he did his best thinking in the darkness of a cold room and thought about what he was going to do now. If they really did fix his belly, he'd have to no longer be nice to people. He didn't want that kind of pain again. People were just going to have to live with it or not. Frankly, he didn't care what people thought about him after this.

Waking up again, he was told he'd have to stay

awake for a little while. He didn't think that was right when he was still hurting, but he didn't say anything. The people at the hospital had done him a solid by taking care of his ulcer, and he was going to be grateful for a long time. He might even donate some money to them for a wing named for him. Yes, he thought, that's what he'd do. Donate enough money to have the hospital beholden to him.

Dismayed to find out that the surgery had been three days ago, he wondered what sort of shit he'd missed. He had things to do now that he was awake enough to get a phone to his ear, and he wasn't getting things done fast enough to suit him. His idea of having a wing named after him was waning now that they were keeping him awake, and he wanted to sue them for not doing their jobs. People were just out for his money, and he didn't like it.

He finally had to reduce himself to begging for a phone so that he could call his daughter to have her get her ass into gear. This surgery made him realize that he was going to die sometime, and he didn't like that either. He wanted to live forever, and the sooner he figured out how to make that work, the better off the people around him would be. Damn it, but he hated that he was so weak, too.

The doctor came in once and told him about the surgery. He was so pissed off that he barely paid attention to what he was saying. Something about him having to have training in how to take care of himself, and that as soon as he was on solid foods, then they'd talk again. Cutting him off, he told him what he wanted.

"I want a phone and a computer brought in here for my use." He said that he'd have to wait a couple more days before he cut him off again. "No, I won't have to wait. You've fixed things up for me, and now I need to get my businesses caught up with. You bring those items in for me so that I can contact my daughter."

"She was notified when you were out of surgery." He asked where she was if she knew. "I'm sure I don't know, sir, but she was notified. She came in right after you were waking up, but I believe she left right after. There were words exchanged between the two of you, and she left here crying."

"I don't believe you. Well, maybe I do. Women cry at the stupidest things. Call her again and tell her that I want to see her. She can even bring that husband of hers if she has to. So long as he remains human. I don't want him coming in here shifting again unless I need him to be something else."

"I'll call, but she said not to call her again unless you were dead. And she seemed serious about that." He said he didn't care; he wanted her there, no matter if he had to send an officer to get her ass down here.

"As I said, I'd call, but I'd not count on her coming. The two of you had an argument, and she went home."

"I'll be the judge of what sort of argument we had." That had made more sense in his head, but he dared the man to say anything. "Just tell her that I said to get her ass down here now. I have things to talk to her about."

When the doctor left, he had to ask for something for pain again. He didn't know what they'd given him, but it didn't put him out like before. Good. Howard wanted to be wide awake when his daughter came around. He was going to have to tell her a few things about her life from now on.

Chapter 10

Devlin didn't mind going to the hospital to talk to Howard. The man had made Sen cry, and that was enough for him to tell the man off. However, he was going to be professional about it when he told the man to fuck off and leave his sister-in-law alone. Smiling, he wondered if he could actually pull it off, but wasn't going to try very hard.

He made it to the room, but the man wasn't there. He'd been taken to x-ray to find out if he'd busted any stitches in his belly when he'd tried to swing at a nurse for telling him that he needed to try and keep off the pain medications a little more.

Devlin had never cared for the man. He'd be polite to him, but he never thought that man was showing his true colors. It was something that he'd learned in being an attorney. He'd tried to tell his brother, but Ivan had said that he was going through a lot and made excuses for him. Now all he could do was tell him how much he wished that he'd listened to him. It made everyone upset that he'd made Sen cry when he had. And continued to do so.

Hearing him coming down the hallway yelling

and ordering people around, Devlin sat in the room's only chair and waited. Once they got him hooked up to all the monitors in his room, the staff left, but he stayed where he was. It took the older man a few minutes to realize that he wasn't alone in the room, but Devlin had heard plenty. The man really was showing himself now, and he wondered why no one else had noticed it.

"Who the hell are you?" Devlin smiled, knowing that the man knew who he was. He'd been to dinner with him several times over the past month. "What do you want? Where is my daughter? She was supposed to be here when I got back, and I demand that you tell her that she's to come and see me. I have things that I want to discuss with her."

"She's not coming." He waited until he finished cursing before he stood up. "You said some things to her when she was here the last time, and she said to tell you that she wants nothing to do with you right now. Perhaps when you're better, but not now."

"Where does she get off telling me anything like that? I'm her father, and she'll do what I said. It's high time she started listening to me or else." Devlin didn't bother pointing out that she was a grown woman and he'd had nothing to do with her since she'd been a baby, but waited on the man to calm down again. "You tell her if she doesn't get her ass down here and talk to me, I'm going to cut her out of my will. Then where will she be?"

"Still quite wealthy, I would imagine. Not to mention happier." He started cursing at him again, and Devlin stood up to leave. He didn't have to take this kind of abuse and told the man that. "I have better things to do than to sit around talking to a bully. And that's what you are. Did you actually tell her that you were sick of being nice to her when all you wanted was for her to take over your businesses? That's not very nice of you if you were to ask me."

"No one asked you. And I don't know what I said to her, but it was probably the truth. Being nice to her was what got me into this hospital in the first place. She should be happy that I'm able to be myself again. All that pussy footing around is what made me sick, and I'm not going to be that way again." Devlin pointed out that he should have been nice because it was the right thing to do. "No, by god, it's not. I'll be the man that I am forever now, and she'll just have to get used to it. I'm not going to allow her or anyone to treat me as if I were nothing to them. You tell her what I said."

"I will, but I don't think it's going to make any difference to her. She's stubborn and right in this case." Howard huffed and clutched his chest. "Did they tell you that you have heart troubles? You should take better care of yourself before you're dead from a heart attack. It could happen with the way that you're going. Then where will you be with all your money but six feet under? If I were you, I'd change my will around now if you're thinking of taking Sen out of your will. Not that she'll mind all that much. Her uncle and aunt left her with enough money to make sure she's happy for the rest of her life."

"Robert was a sap. He told me to stay out of her life from the very beginning if I didn't want a good relationship with her." Devlin said he sounded like a smart man. "Shows what you know. I told him he wasn't to leave her any of his estate either. I wanted her to be beholden to me. So what does he do? He goes ahead and leaves her everything that he had. If he were here right now, I'd take him to task. There was no point in leaving her anything when I had more money than he did."

"I don't think that the fact that he left her money had to do with anything. You're just jealous that he got to leave her anything that would cut you out of the picture. I would have liked that man had he not died. I think we could have been good friends." Howard told him to shut up. "I will, but only because I'm leaving. If you want to have anything to do with Sen again, I suggest that you be the man that she knew before you got sick."

He was clutching his chest when he left the

room. It would be just like the man to be on life support for the rest of his natural life, and the only one that could pull the plug would be Sen. Wouldn't that be about the funniest thing that ever happened?

As he headed to the elevator, he thought about the conversation that he'd had with Howard. The man really was off his head if he thought that any of them would allow him to talk to Sen the way that he did for a second time. Especially Ivan. He'd been angry enough to want to come down to the hospital and rip his throat out. He might just end up doing that for the way that he'd treated his mate, and there wouldn't be a single member of the family who would tell him he'd been wrong. Sen had cried for hours after leaving the hospital.

The very fact that he didn't remember the conversation that he'd had with her showed what sort of man he was. He'd not bothered with any of the details of what he'd said to her, and that pissed him off enough that he'd like to be the one who ripped his throat out. It would serve him right if the entire family had something to do with his demise.

Devlin was just getting off the elevator when he heard the code blue being called. He didn't remember the room number that Howard was in, but he knew that it was right around the four-hundred number. Thinking about the man having a heart attack right now made him smile. It served him right that he'd die today instead of after he got his will changed around. Sen was going to be a very, very wealthy woman if he were the man they were calling the code for.

He didn't bother hanging around to find out but went home. He was going to stop by Ivan and Sen's house on the way home to tell them how it went, but he would not mention the code being called. He wasn't sure that it was for the man, and he didn't want to get their hopes up. He knew that Sen would mourn the loss of her father; it's the way that it should have been. But he doubted very much there would be too many tears shed in his honor, like the man would hope for. Or demand, for that matter.

Telling them what the man had said was easier because Sen had told him to tell her exactly what was said. Not that he could lie to her, but he would have liked to have sugar-coated it a bit. She didn't deserve the words that had come out of the older man's mouth to be repeated to her, and he told her that.

"I should have listened to what you had to say to me when you told me that he was faking his demeanor. You had a better handle on him than the rest of us did, and I can't thank you enough for telling me that. I didn't listen, but at least I know that he didn't fool all of us. You're a good man, Devlin. And I'm ever so grateful that you went there to talk to him." The house phone was ringing when he told her that it had been his pleasure. "That has to be the hospital. They're the only ones with that number."

After getting off the phone with the call, it was indeed the hospital, and Sen was told that her father had had a massive coronary event. While he had a good guess as to what that meant, the man had died in the hospital. Sen didn't seem to be too terribly upset about it now, but he knew that once she thought of it, it would weigh heavily on her mind and heart. She was tender-hearted like that, and he knew that they'd all be there for her.

"The nurse said that he was told to calm himself down a bit or he'd pull out the stitches. I don't know what happened to upset him so much, but I can well imagine that it didn't take much. He seemed to me like he enjoyed being angry all the time." Devlin agreed with her, and Ivan said that he was sure that it didn't take much to make him angry when he was in a good mood, too. "I can believe that. When I was in there talking to him, he seemed to want to pick a fight with me all the time. Like if he wasn't picking at me, he'd pick at the nurses. I would have thought they were the wrong people to fight with when they could withhold his medications."

"One of the nurses told Howard that he needed to back off on the painkillers. He was taking them for the slightest pains. That's not the way that she said it, of course, but you could tell that it didn't make him happy at all to be told no on something." Devlin looked at Ivan when he spoke about the argument that he'd had with the doctors. "I heard about that. He was telling them that he knew more about medicine than they ever would and that his body was a temple. The man had to be a hundred pounds overweight, and he told us that he had high blood pressure."

"Stupid person." Sen sat down on the couch next to Ivan and smiled. "I don't know how I feel about him being dead yet. I know that he was my father, but for the most part, he had nothing to do with raising me. Neither did my mother, for that matter. She stayed out of my life until I was older, and that suited me just fine."

"I'm here for you if you need anything. So you know, he did tell me that if you didn't do what he wanted, he was going to take you out of the will. I've not seen it as yet, but I would imagine that he had a lot of hoops you would have had to go through to get the money in the first place. You might be better off if he had taken you out." She told them that she didn't care one way or the other. Her uncle had left her well off, and she didn't have any worries. "But for your mom. We'll have to see what happens when she get out of jail. I have no idea what sort of demands she's going to put on you about him, but I think I'd be prepared if I were you."

"I will be. I think over the last several days I've been shown a lot of things that I didn't know before. Like the temperament of my father, for sure, but also my mother. I think I'm going to be washing my hands of her as well before this is all over. She's told several people at the jail that she wants me dead, not to mention a few of the officers who are there. That has to carry some weight, don't you think?" Devlin said he'd try to get her a longer stay, but didn't know who the judge was. "If it's Rainer, then I think he'll believe me when I tell him that she's threatened me."

"He might not be able to be there for you at all. He's too close to you, so that would make it a conflict of interest on his part." She said she'd never thought of that. "I don't know how it works with judges. I've personally never run into that kind of situation before. However, lawyers can't, and I'm sure you have heard that before working where you do."

"I think you might be right. I remember looking into that once for one of the other partners. The judge said that he wasn't able to try the case because of his sister-in-law being a part of the defendant's case." She looked like she was thinking hard on something, and he let her while he spoke to his brother. When she spoke then, she remembered the case. "No, I'm sure that a judge would have to recuse himself from a case since I work for him. That might come back to bite him in the ass if he were to do that."

"Then she'll have to wait until another judge can take her case. That could take a while." She asked if she'd have to stay in jail while they waited on that. "That I know for sure. Yes, she'll have to wait until some judge can preside over her case without any troubles. That could be as much as another month. Or longer." She said she would hope for that. "Don't rely on me for being right on that. I've seen where a judge could come from another county to do a case just because the first judge was ill. It will depend on the caseload of the second judge."

"Well, I don't care. I hope she has to stay in jail for a long time." Sen stood up, and the two of them did as well. "I need to take a nap. I've enjoyed taking a snooze in the afternoon, so I'm going to go up and try to rest. You two have fun."

After she was gone, Ivan watched her as she walked away. Devlin said his name twice before he turned and looked at him. He asked if she was going to be all right. Shrugging, he said that he didn't know for sure, but he thought that she was better than she'd ever been.

"That's good." Ivan said it was and smiled at him. "You're looking sappy again. What's going on with you? Did you deliver any more puppies?"

"Yes, as a matter of fact, I did, but that's not what has me 'sappy' as you called it. I just realized how much I love my mate. And yours is out there waiting to make you just as sappy." He said that he didn't want to be sappy all the time. "It's a great feeling. One that I hope you have on your face for the rest of your life. It'll suit you, little brother, and I hope she's just as sappy as you are."

~*~

"I'm going to kill her and her husband off as soon as I get out of here. She should have come to see me at least once a day since I've been in here. There is no telling what she's done with his money without me around to make sure that she doesn't spend it willy nilly like she does." However, Debra knew in her mind that Sen never spent a dime willy nilly; it was her that spent money stupidly. "But hey, once I get it, I'm going to be on easy street."

"So you keep saying." The officer had brought her something to eat and hadn't walked away when she started talking to her. It was all right with her. Debra was getting sick of her own company and needed someone to pay attention to her. "There's extras today if you want them. I have extra cake and sandwiches to have. But you can't have both. Decide now so that I can let the other officer know which one you're taking."

"The cake." Nodding, the officer left her to her meal. They weren't that bad, but she always thought that there could have been more of it. Breakfast was plentiful, but lunch was a lot to be desired. It was usually one sandwich with a piece of fruit and a slice of pie or cake. She could have all the coffee or tea she wanted, but it was like drinking sludge, and she didn't want more than a cupful with her meal. "You'd think they'd want to take better care of me since I'm going to have all that money."

She didn't know how she'd gotten it in her head that her brother had left Sen a great deal of money. He'd never acted like he had anything more than a hundred bucks on him at any time. It was more than she had on her, of course, but he never had credit cards on him. He'd told her once that he didn't believe in paying for things on credit, so he didn't have any. Everybody had credit cards. Even she had them, and she was broke all the time.

Debra thought about the last time she'd spoken to her brother. It had been a fight as usual, but this time it wasn't about Sen but money. He'd told her that she had plenty enough coming to her, and without any kind of house payment or utilities, she should be on easy street. Perhaps he was right, and she should have been, but she so liked to spend money. And she thought that she was really good at it, too.

Laughing to herself, she thought of the look on Robert's face when she told him how broke she was by the end of the month. He tried to tell her that the money wasn't going to last forever, she'd better be saving a bit of it back so she'd have something to live on. She'd tried that once, and it didn't work out for her. Being on a budget was something that she'd never learned. Now that the money had dried up, she'd rather kill someone than have to work out a way to have spendable money all the time. Sen should have been taking care of her.

Debra didn't have any friends. She knew people, but she'd not depend on them to come and help her if she was in a jam. Sometimes that was just sad to her that she didn't have anyone that she could depend on, but she'd get paid again, and all thoughts of having lunch with someone other than Sen would go away. But of late, Sen wouldn't have lunch with her either. Something about rent being due or something along those lines.

Whatever. She was going to get out of here, then she'd be as rich as her brother had been. Or at least she hoped so. Whatever Robert had left Sen, he should have known that she'd put up a fuss about it and would have to kill her daughter. It would be his fault too if she ended up killing her, and she'd not go to jail. He should have known that she'd do anything to get to the money. She'd knocked him around enough for it.

But that hadn't worked out for her either. Debra had spent a month in jail when she'd knocked him around. And had his hospital bills taken out of her next check before it ever got to her. Which didn't help her situation out at all when she was broke all the time.

She never really beat him, but did use a ball bat on him when she'd been there that day. She'd been pissed off that none of his mail had *past due* written on it. All of her credit card statements had that written on them every month. That's when he told her that he didn't have any credit cards and had never used credit at all. If he wanted something, he paid for it. She did the same thing, but after a few weeks of having something that she thought she wanted, it was no longer shiny to her. That was how she came to be broke all the time and her credit cards past due. She just loved to spend money.

"Here's your cake. That's all there is left, so don't ask me for anything else." She promised she wouldn't, but knew that she would. It was like her to have to ask several times for something and never get it. These people were holding back on her, and she didn't like it. "Also, you won't be going to court with the others tomorrow. Something about a conflict of interest where the judge is concerned. You'll have to wait on someone else to come in and take the case for you."

"No, that's not right. I don't care about a conflict.

You tell him, since I don't care, then it shouldn't matter to him." She told her that it didn't work like that. "I don't care. They can't have me sitting in here like I don't have shit to do all the time waiting on him to get off his ass and get me out of here. I've done nothing wrong."

"I'm not the judge that hears you. You'll have to take it up with him." She said she would tomorrow. "You're not going to unless you have his phone number and a phone, you're not going to be able to get in touch with him. Your family has been notified as well."

"They're the ones that put me in here. Why do any of them care that I'm in here? They're not the ones wasting time sitting on their asses." She just knew that Sen was spending her money too. She'd already bought herself a new home and put stuff in it. It had been in the newspaper the other day when she'd gotten to glance at it. "I will be going tomorrow and talking to this judge. He's going to release me so that I can get on with the things I want to get finished. My daughter is out there spending my money like it belongs to her, and I won't have it. Promise me that you'll make sure that I get out of here in the morning, and I'll pay you well for it. As soon as I get my money that should have come to me in the first place, you'll be the first one I pay back."

"No." When she walked away, Debra could

have spit. She did that to people when words failed her. But they told her that if she spit once more while in the system, they were going to tape her mouth closed. She didn't know if they could do that or not, but she wasn't taking any chances. Police in small towns had their own set of rules they followed, and she knew better than to fuck with them.

When her meal tray was taken from her, she noticed that it wasn't the same officer. She didn't want to get into things with someone else, so she just handed over her tray and said nothing. Tomorrow, she was going to have to figure out how to get to the courthouse before Sen spent all her money. It hadn't been fair of her brother to leave his money to Sen, and she was willing to kill her for it. Brother and sister had a tighter bond than uncle to niece, and she was going to make sure that Sen knew that.

"I'll kill her, and no one will care." She thought about how she was going to do that since they'd taken her gun from her. She didn't have any money coming in to buy another one either, since Howard had put those rules in place, and now she was without a house and money. She missed her car, too. Being able to drive herself around to get things when she wanted them had been a pleasure that she'd not realized that she liked. "Now that's all gone because of my dumbass daughter. Sen should have learned not to mess with me when I'm right. That money is all mine."

She tried to think what she'd done with the first bit of money she'd gotten from Robert's estate. Nothing came to mind. She certainly hadn't paid any bills with it. It was like free money, and she was going to spend it as she saw fit. And she did. Right up until all ten grand of it was gone, and she had less than fifty bucks in her pocket. That last bit of money had gone for her gun. Now the police had that as well.

At dinner time, she was brought another tray of food. Tonight was pasta and marinara sauce. She asked if there was anything extra and was told to eat what she got. Debra liked to make herself pasta sandwiches with the garlicy bread with the noodles and sauce dripping down the sides. It was her favorite way to eat pasta. Tonight, with only one slice of the bread, she was going to have to make do. She missed the other officer; she always made sure there were extras for her.

Disappointed in her meal, she didn't care for the cake that she was given either; she was still hungry when she was told to hand over her empty tray. Begging for something more to eat with the promise of money when she got out got her nowhere but an empty belly and nothing to show for it. Debra hated that she was reduced to paying anyone extra for anything, and it pissed her off when no one took her seriously. She wanted her money, by god.

When the lights were turned out, a stupid thing to do, she thought, she was left alone with her thoughts. Plotting the way that she always was, she wondered how she could get Sen by herself so that she could get her money. She wasn't above killing her for the money, but perhaps she would just hand it over without any trouble. Probably not. She certainly wouldn't.

Then she'd have to kill that husband of hers. If she were really married. That way he couldn't get what should have been hers in the first place. Debra knew that she might have to spend a couple more days in jail until they figured out that the money did indeed belong to her and that Sen had caused her to kill her. That man, she didn't know his name, who was supposed to be her husband, would have to die too, and that too would be Robert's fault for not giving it to her in the first place.

It did occur to her that there might not be any money to be had. Robert always acted like he didn't have a penny to his name. But there were times when she was sure that he had more than he was saying, like the time she'd been invited to his birthday party one year when Sen had been little. The bash was huge, and there had been plenty of food to go around. Even the gifts that had been displayed on the big table had been expensive. He had more than he let on simply because he didn't want her to have it.

"Bastard." She was told to be quiet. Lights out meant that it was quiet time, too. Like she cared. She did her best plotting while it was in the dark of the night, and she would have them so worked out that they would go flawlessly when she was ready to do them. Getting the money from Sen was going to be no different. As soon as she saw her daughter again, she was going to make sure that she understood that when it happened to her, her being killed because of the money, it was because of Robert. Then let her think that her saintly uncle was all that nice when he was going to cause her and her husband's death.

She knew that she was going to need a weapon. Debra had been told she wasn't going to be reimbursed for the weapon that they took from her. Something about a parole violation. Just how long was she supposed to follow those rules was something that she'd ask, and since she didn't care for the answer of all the time, Debra had ignored it. That's the way she'd done all the rules when she didn't like them, and it had served her well up until now. No one was giving her gun back to her.

Thinking about giving money to one of the officers for their gun had some merit, but she didn't see them just handing it over without cash up front. They were very careful about their weapons, too, never having them on them when they came back to bring her anything that she'd had coming to her. Like they didn't trust her or something.

"When I get out of here, I'm going to have to kill more people than I first thought when things don't go my way." There were two of the officers that she wanted dead simply because they looked down on her when they were bringing her a tray. Then there was the daughter and husband who would have to die. "I'm going to need some more ammo, too, if my list gets any longer."

Being told to shut up again, she simply rolled to her side. It was better than engaging in a heated conversation with the man up the row from her. He might well be on her list, too, before this was all done. Shooting her way out of jail did have some appeal. Especially since Robert was going to be taking the blame for all of it.

Before You Go...

HELP AN AUTHOR

write a review

THANK YOU!

Share your voice and help guide other readers to these wonderful books. Even if it's only a line or two, your reviews help readers discover the author's books so they can continue creating stories that you'll love. Log in to your favorite retailer and leave a review. Thank you.

AWARD WINNING, BESTSELLING AUTHOR

Kathi S. Barton is an award-winning and bestselling author known for her steamy paranormal romances and unforgettable characters. A recipient of the prestigious Pinnacle Book Achievement Award, her books have topped the charts on Amazon and All Romance eBooks, earning her a loyal global readership.

Kathi lives in Nashport, Ohio, with her husband, Paul. When she's not crafting passionate love stories set in magical worlds, she enjoys camping, exploring local auctions, and attending county fairs, where Paul showcases his artwork and pottery. Her creative spark — fueled by a muse she describes as a cross between Jimmy Stewart and Hugh Jackman — brings her stories to vivid, heartfelt life.

Paranormal romance with plenty of heat is her favorite genre, and she loves connecting with her readers. Feel free to reach out — Kathi would love to hear from you.

Email: aaronskiss@gmail.comFollow Kathi on her blog: http:// kathisbartonauthor.blogspot.com/

www.ingramcontent.com/pod-product-compliance
Lightning Source LLC
Chambersburg PA
CBHW031959170626
46807CB00006B/2562